THE GIRL ON
RUSK STREET

Penny Carlile

For Steve

"Do not be overcome by evil, but overcome evil with good."
Romans 12:21

JUNE 1960

"Kee-Wo-Kee-K-A-T! Kee-Wo-Kee-K-A-T!" I yelled from the bottom of the steps. My best friend, Katie Baxter, lived in the two-story house across from my home on Rusk Street. I fidgeted as I picked at the peeling white paint on the wooden banister that led to the Baxters' second floor apartment. Katie, her mama, daddy and little sister Annie lived above her grandparents in a big house with a silver blue wrap-around porch.

Summer was finally here. Almost three full months with no homework, no spelling bees, no story problems and no geography lessons. Summer meant kickball and hide 'n seek and bike rides to Asaffs to buy popsicles for a nickel.

I called out for Katie again. The summer of 1960 would be like all summers on Rusk Street. We'd build a fort, swing in the hammock, sell homemade pot holders and cook eggs on the sidewalk.

Katie threw open the screen door and bounded down the stairs two at a time. A carbon copy of her mother Mavis, Katie was short-waisted, chubby and a good six inches shorter than I was. She had a wide smile and blonde wispy hair that was parted down the middle. Her glasses sat a little crooked on her nose. She greeted me with a thin ring of milk around her mouth.

"Race you to the swing!" I said as soon as Katie's right foot touched the bottom step. It was not really a fair race since I was two years older than Katie and was also the fastest girl in our elementary school. Only Dennis Alexander was faster than me in a foot race at our end of school track meet, and he was part Cherokee Indian. I always beat Katie to the wooden swing on her grandparents' porch. I hopped in first and waited for Katie to join me before we pushed off with our feet and heard the ceiling above us creak and groan as the heavy silver chains held fast to the old white swing.

"Let's plan our day." I loved to organize. Mama told me that planning was one of the gifts the Lord had given me and that I should always use my gifts to the best of my ability.

"Hmm," responded Katie who was more a thinker than a planner. "I wanna draw a picture of the sky. It's so blue."

Katie had already decided that she wanted to be an art teacher when she grew up. Her mother taught second grade at Davy Crockett Elementary and had asked our principal at Stephen F. Austin to let Katie take a test to see if she could skip a grade. I wouldn't want to be the youngest kid in my class, but Katie was excited that she would only be one grade behind Lawrence Miller and me.

Lawrence, who was known by practically everyone as Law, lived next door to Katie and across Rusk Street from me with his grandmother, Martha Lawrence. Law's mother, Charla, was the only divorced person I knew. She and Law had lived with Mrs. Lawrence for as long as I had known Law until last Christmas. That's when Charla married a man named Roy Ed Peteet and moved to his apartment. Law's mother let him decide if he wanted to move in with them or stay with his grandmother. He stayed.

Law had asthma, and his dark brown eyes watered because of his allergies. He had a pet squirrel named Alvin who lived in a cage inside his house. Law found Alvin in his front yard three years ago. He was a baby squirrel then, so his mother and grandmother let Law take care of him. Alvin didn't seem to make Law's allergies any worse. Law was an only child, and Alvin kept him company. Law's dark hair was always slicked down with Vitalis. He was my boyfriend even though he let me boss him around.

Katie and I were still sitting in the porch swing when Law opened his back door and walked over our way.

"Whatcha doin'?" he asked.

"Plannin' our day. I wanna climb the mimosa tree. Katie wants to draw a picture. Whatta you wanna do?"

"Build a fort."

Law loved building forts. Every summer we picked a different place. From our fort we could watch out for bad guys and warn all of the neighbors.

"I found the best place," Law said as he pointed toward the corner. "Behind the Fowlers' house. Nobody lives there since they moved. Back in the woods it's dark, and nobody can see us. They even have a garage if we wanna take turns sittin' on the roof watchin' for robbers."

As I jumped from the swing and ran down the front porch steps, I yelled, "Let's go see it."

Katie and Law followed behind me. My long brown hair was in a ponytail. Most days I left my house before mama had a chance to tie a ribbon around it. Daddy called me his tomboy. Daddy was the head football coach at Marshall High School. He was hoping for a son when I was born. That's why my parents named me Roberta so that Daddy could call me Bobbi. He taught me to throw a baseball, kick a football and roll the best baby bouncers in our kickball games. I loved being outdoors. My olive skin got dark each summer, and every August Daddy would say that I'd better not get any darker or some people would think I was a colored child. Mama told him to hush when he said that. I had large green eyes, skinny

3

arms and long legs. I also talked a lot and asked more questions than Mama wanted to answer. She had her hands full looking after my little sister, Betsy.

Law was right. The woods behind the old Fowler house were perfect for a fort. The three of us crawled through some vines to reach a nice cool patch of dirt. Tall pine trees and smaller oak trees grew around a dry creek bed. We could build the best fort ever with sticks and rocks and pieces of wood that Daddy had left outside his tool shed. No one would even know we were there. I was already planning how the fort would look.

"You think they'll care?" asked Katie.

"No one lives here," I answered.

"They can't even see us," said Law. "Watch. I'll go out there in the backyard and look."

Law crawled on his stomach through the vines. When he stood up, his striped t-shirt was dirty. Mrs. Lawrence wouldn't be happy about that.

"I can't see you," he called out to us. "Even your white hair doesn't show," he said to Katie.

"My hair isn't white. It's blonde. Don't boys know anything?" she asked me.

I shrugged. "Let's find some sticks and rocks. This'll be the greatest fort ever," I told them.

We worked all morning and were dirty and tired when I heard my mother calling,

"Bobbi! Lunch!"

"See ya after lunch," I said to the others as I crawled out through the vines.

As I came around the corner of the empty Fowler house, I saw a large white truck moving slowly down our street. I read the big black letters on the side of the truck—K. L. Dunn Transfer and Storage.

⟨⟩

Mama put my plate on the table. A peanut butter and jelly sandwich with no edges. This truly was a great summer already. My favorite sandwich and a great place for a new fort, too.

"Mama, what is K. L. Dunn Transfer and Storage?" I asked between bites.

She was holding my one-year-old sister on one hip and was trying to get her to finish a cup of milk. "It's a movin' company. They store people's furniture at their warehouse over on Bomar, but they also move people's belongings from one town to another. Why'd you ask about them?"

"I saw their truck when I was comin' home. It was drivin' real slow like the driver was lookin' for somebody."

"I'll take a look," she said as she headed into the small formal living room at the front of our house. She pulled back the curtains and looked through the window. When she didn't see anything, she opened the front door and stepped out onto our narrow front porch with Betsy still on her hip.

"They stopped all right. At the corner in front of the Fowler place," she called to me.

I jumped up from the table and ran to the front door. "Why that house?" I was thinking about our new fort.

"That's the only empty house on the street. I suppose someone might be movin' in. Nice to have new neighbors." Mama loved to meet people.

"Thanks for lunch. I gotta go tell Katie and Law." I ran back toward our new fort.

Katie and Law weren't back at the fort yet, so I decided to walk along the black top road that ran beside the Fowler house. I could see the driver sitting in the moving truck smoking a cigarette. He was talking to another man who kept looking out his window.

I hurried back to the fort. No one was there. I ran across the street and around to the back of Law's house. No one ever went to Law's front door. I didn't know why except that there were two really big magnolia trees in his front yard. Maybe people couldn't see his front door. I knocked on the back door. Mrs. Lawrence opened the screen door and frowned. She was a small lady with white hair that she pulled straight back into a small bun. She was wearing a floral printed cotton dress and glasses that were perched on the end of her nose. She always looked worried. I thought that she was probably worried about Law's allergies. She sat by the front bedroom window crocheting every day. She said that window had good light from the south, but I knew it was really so she could keep an eye on Law and on everybody else on Rusk Street, too.

"Hi, Mrs. Lawrence. Can Law come out?" I asked and smiled my biggest smile.

"He hasn't finished his lunch, but you can come in." She held the screen door open for me.

Law was at his kitchen table eating a mayonnaise sandwich. Some of the mayonnaise was sticking to his left cheek. He loved mayonnaise sandwiches.

"Guess what I saw," I whispered to him.

"What?"

"A movin' truck's parked in front of the Fowlers' house."

"What'd you say about a movin' truck?" asked Mrs. Lawrence who was washing dishes in the sink. Daddy said that old people couldn't hear very well, but Mrs. Lawrence could always hear us even if we were whispering.

"A movin' truck," I told her excitedly. "It's parked right out on the street. If you look out the front window, you can see it."

She walked into their dark sitting room, pulled back the cotton curtains and peered out the window. I followed her to the window.

"I think the men are havin' their lunch in the truck," I whispered.

She grabbed her heart and said, "Oh, child, I didn't know you were there. You gave me a scare."

6

"Sorry, Mrs. Lawrence. Did you see it?"

"I did," she said and frowned again. "I hope the new people aren't rowdy. We don't need rowdy around here."

Law came into the room. "I wanna see."

"Finish your lunch first," Mrs. Lawrence told him. "Then you can go with Bobbi."

"I'm finished, Meme."

"Wash the mayonnaise off your face and finish your milk. Don't forget to take your pill," she reminded him.

"I hate pills," he muttered.

"It's not good to hate," I told him. "Mama says that hatin' just makes the hater's heart hurt."

Law swallowed his pill.

We heard a knock at the back door. Katie was standing there when Mrs. Lawrence opened the screen door. Law and I darted out to meet her. As we walked around to the front yard, Katie asked, "Y'all see it?"

"It's a really big truck. I hope the new people have kids."

"What about the fort?" Law asked as our tennis shoes made a crunching sound on the gravel driveway.

"What about it?" I turned to look at him.

"It's in their backyard," he said.

"Not really." I shook my head. "It's behind their yard back in the trees. That's really nobody's yard. Anyway, I don't think they'll care. Colonel Alton let us build a fort behind his house last summer. He never fussed at us, and we even pretended to shoot him when he was gettin' out of his car."

A large tan car that looked like a tank pulled up behind the moving truck.

Katie, Law and I looked at each other. Must be the new neighbors. We sat down on the curb to watch.

The car door swung open, and a tall woman with long red hair stepped out. She was wearing a white sundress, brown sunglasses and red high heels. Her red lipstick matched the red and yellow scarf she had tied around her hair.

"Who's that?" Law asked.

"She's really pretty," said Katie.

"She looks like a movie star," I told them.

The two men opened their doors and climbed out of the moving truck. The lady with red hair said something to them and pointed at the house where the Fowlers used to live.

"She must be the new neighbor," I said.

"How can you tell?" Law asked.

"She's tellin' them where to put stuff. See."

The lady was talking to the movers. They had unlatched the back door of their truck and were starting to unload a wooden table and chairs. I could see lamps, rugs, a mattress and a big piano inside the truck plus stacks of cardboard boxes.

"I don't see any toys."

"Me either," said Katie, disappointed.

"Let's go talk to her." I started across the road.

"We might bother her," said Law.

"I bet we won't."

Katie walked beside me. Law followed a few steps behind.

The tall lady saw us and turned around.

"Hey," I said and gave a little wave from below my waist.

"Hello," she said with a big smile. "Do you children live around here?"

"In that house with the pink shutters," I said and pointed toward my house.

Katie said, "I live in that big white house."

Law was acting shy, but he finally spoke up, "Across the street. Right there."

"Oh, I love magnolia trees! Is that your house with those beautiful trees?"

"Yes, ma'am."

"What nice manners you have, young man," she said as she smiled at Law. "My name is Lucille Harris, but your mothers will probably want you to call me Miss Lucille even though I'm only twenty-five."

"I'm Bobbi," I said and gave her another little wave. "She's Katie, and he's Law. Are you movin' in the Fowlers' house?"

"If that's who lived here before me, I am," she laughed. "These nice men have been waiting for me to let them in." She waved to them, and the men smiled back at her. "I guess I better open the door."

She seemed to glide up the front walk to the door. I had never seen anyone in person like Miss Lucille Harris. She was beautiful. Her skin was very white, and her wavy hair was the color of a fire engine. She took the scarf off of her head. I could tell that the men moving furniture from the truck to her house thought that she was pretty, too. They were staring at her. We followed her to the porch.

"You have any kids?" Katie finally worked up the nerve to ask.

"Oh, honey, I don't," she said. "It's just me. I had a husband, but...."

She stopped in the middle of the sentence like she had forgotten something. Then she said, "My husband died. I came here to teach at the college. I better get to work helping these nice gentlemen. See you around," she said and waved to us over her shoulder.

"No kids," Katie said.

"I think maybe she's a movie star. We never met a movie star before," I told them. "Let's go to the fort and watch."

By late afternoon the movers closed the doors of their truck, climbed back in the cab and drove away. From our fort we could see Lucille Harris through her kitchen window. The window was open, and she was humming as she unpacked a box of dishes.

"Bobbi! Supper!" called Mama.

"See ya tomorrow," I said to Katie. Law had already left. He was bored watching our new neighbor, so he had gone home to feed Alvin.

9

"I'm comin', too," said Katie as she fell in step with me. "That's a really big piano for such a little house."

"I'm gonna ask Mama to bake Miss Lucille a pie. She likes to bake pies for people."

━━◄‡ ‡►━━

"Just a minute," Lucille Harris called from somewhere in the back of her house.

Mama had Betsy on her left hip as she knocked on the front door. I was holding a warm chocolate pie that was one of Mama's specialties.

"No hurry," answered Mama.

As Miss Lucille came to the door, she was tugging on the waist of her navy blue pedal pushers with her left hand and wiping her forehead with the back of her right hand. Her red hair was pulled back in a ponytail like mine. She was wearing bright red lipstick.

"I've been unpacking. It gets really warm in that back bedroom. I may have to buy a window unit to cool it down. Come on in," she said as she held open the screen door.

"Mama baked this for you. It's chocolate." I handed her the pie.

"That's mighty nice of you," she said and looked at Mama. "I'm Lucille."

"I'm Juanita Rogers. Everybody calls me Nita. Welcome to Rusk Street."

"This pie smells delicious." She smiled. "Please sit down if you can find a spot. Let me move this box and make some room for you on the couch. How old's your baby?"

We sat down on the couch which was covered with pretty pink flowers. It wasn't soft like our old brown couch. The hard back made me sit up straight. Mama was wearing pink shorts, a pink blouse and white tennis shoes. She matched Miss Lucille's floral

10

couch. Mama's hair was brown—she called it mousy brown—and wasn't as thick as mine. She rolled it every night on pink sponge rollers and got a permanent wave a few times a year to help keep the curl in. She was so busy cooking, cleaning and chasing Betsy around that she had lost most of her baby weight. Daddy always said that his favorite thing about Mama was her big smile. She was a happy person.

"She just had her first birthday, and Bobbi's ten. Course, she's prob'ly told you that already. My Bobbi never met a stranger."

"I met Bobbi and her friends day before yesterday. Very friendly children."

I smiled at her.

"Bobbi tells me that you're plannin' to teach at the college. Jack and I, Jack's my husband, know several of the teachers there. They say it's a good place to work. Nice Baptist folks and all," said Mama. Betsy was squirming in her lap.

"I hope so. It will be a little different for me—my first time to work with a lot of colored people."

I saw Mama's eyes get big.

Miss Lucille noticed them, too, and said, "Bishop's where I'll be working. You were probably thinking of ETBC."

"I was," said Mama.

"I leased this house thinking I had a job at ETBC, but the job fell through, so I applied at Bishop since it's practically right across the street from here. They called me the day after they received my application in the mail. I came down for an interview and fell in love with Wyalucing. When they offered me a job teaching piano and voice, I signed the contract right away before it could fall through. I figure students are students no matter their color."

While I was playing on the floor with Betsy, I listened to Mama as she told Miss Lucille about ETBC and Bishop.

"Did you know that East Texas Baptist College used to be called College of Marshall? It was built on the highest spot in Harrison

County in 1914. It's a pretty campus. I guess you saw it when you interviewed for a job there."

Miss Lucille nodded.

"It's Southern Baptist, and a good number of the people who teach at the college go to church with us down at First Baptist."

"You sure do know a lot about it," Miss Lucille said to Mama.

"Our neighbor on the other side, Lottie Van Worth, loves history. She told me all about ETBC, Bishop and Wiley—the other colored college in town—when we moved to Rusk Street. And some of it I learned at the church from going to missionary society meetings and such."

"I'm sure Bishop has an interesting history, too," said Miss Lucille.

"It does. Lottie told me that Bishop was started by a man named Nathan Bishop because he wanted a Texas college for colored Baptists. Some local Baptist ministers raised money to buy some land from the Holcomb family. Nathan Bishop's widow later bought forty more acres and gave that land to the school. Somebody told me that she wanted young colored men to be preachers, but I think that they must teach more than preachin' now since you will be teachin' music."

"They have classes like most colleges," said Miss Lucille. Bishop was located catty-cornered from her house. She could walk to her classes.

"I guess they told you all about Wyalucing," said Mama who seemed to have recovered from her surprise that Miss Lucille would be teaching at a colored school.

"Not much, but it's one of the prettiest homes I've ever seen. My classes will be on the second floor. I can look out the window and see those huge magnolia trees."

"Slaves built it, and then some of the former slaves here in Harrison County bought it. The first president of the college lived there."

"Why'd they name it Wyalucing?"

"They say that Lucy Holcombe, the daughter of the family who built it in 1850, was very beautiful, a true Southern belle. She introduced iced tea and silk stockings to the people of Marshall, and I surely do thank her for both of those things. Her daddy named the house after her. It's such a pretty place with those big white columns."

"Have you been inside?"

"Oh, no," Mama said as she shook her head.

"Well, you should. It's just as pretty inside as out."

Mama just smiled.

"Would you like a glass of tea? How about some pink lemonade for the girls?" She asked both questions as she stood up.

"Tea sounds wonderful on this hot day, and I'm sure the girls would love some pink lemonade. Do you have plastic cups—nothin' breakable, please. We'll try not to make a mess. My husband Jack is the head football coach at the high school here. Marshall's a football town."

"I don't know a thing about football. Never been to a game. My late husband was a college professor," she called out from the kitchen.

"I'm sorry to hear about your husband," said Mama.

"He was killed in an awful automobile wreck over in Dallas. That's where we used to live," she said as she handed Mama a glass of sweet tea and then gave Betsy and me plastic cups filled with pink lemonade.

"You wouldn't believe the traffic there. Too many crazy drivers. A man ran a red light and hit William right in the driver's door. He was gone on the spot. Eight months ago now. I still can't believe it. We'd only been married a year and a half. We taught at the same college." She touched her eyes with her napkin. "I have a brother in Houston. He asked me to move in with his family, but I just couldn't live in another big city. I saw the job posting for a music teacher at ETBC on the board at my college. I finished the school year the middle of May, told them why I needed to leave, and here I am." She waved her hands a lot as she talked.

"That's a big piano," I said when she stopped talking to Mama. The piano was in the corner of the room. It was just like the piano at our church. Mama called that one a baby grand.

"I'm planning to give piano lessons here at the house a few afternoons since my college classes end about two each day."

"Can I take piano lessons, Mama?"

"I don't know, Bobbi. Miss Lucille prob'ly just teaches college students."

"Do you like music, Bobbi?"

"I'm a real good singer at school. That's what Mrs. Sherman told the class. Please, Mama, please! Can I take lessons?"

"We'll see," she said as she patted my hand. "I'll need to talk to your daddy about it."

"Tonight?"

"We'll see. Now drink your lemonade, and let us grownups talk. Betsy is getting fidgety, and she'll have to go down for a nap soon."

While we finished our drinks, Mama told Miss Lucille about our neighbors.

"Across Rusk Street are Mrs. Lawrence and her grandson Law. Next to them are the Baxters—Mavis, Howard, Katie, Annie and Howard's parents. Mrs. Lawrence and the Baxters share a gravel driveway and a garage. Jim and Ruth Tressell live across a vacant lot just east of the Baxters. Mr. Tressell works for the railroad and has a big garden behind his house. The Tressells pretty much keep to themselves since Mrs. Tressell's in a wheelchair. Colonel Alton and his wife live farther down the street on that same side, but we don't see them very much since he's in the military." She stopped then to drink some of her tea. "On this side of the street our house is the closest one to yours across the vacant lot. On the other side of our house are Mr. and Mrs. Van Worth and their daughter Lottie who teaches Spanish at the high school. The Sewells live in the two-story white Victorian house on the other side of the Van Worths. Mr. Sewell works at the ammunitions factory. Jack says that he has an important job in management. He tells other people how to make bombs for the army."

"I'll have to get around to meeting all of them. Thank you so much for the pie and the visit," Miss Lucille told Mama as we stood up to leave.

"You're very welcome. Happy to have the chance to visit. If you have any questions about anything in Marshall, just ask. You'll find people for the most part are really nice here."

As we walked home, my mother was humming.

"You like her, Mama?"

"I do. She's very friendly. I hope she likes it here. I just wish the job at ETBC had worked out. I don't think it's good for her to teach at Bishop."

"But she can walk to school. It's so close to her house."

"It may be too close," she said. I wasn't sure what that meant, but for once I didn't ask.

━◦+ +◦━

"Come on in, Bobbi," called Miss Lucille. "Have a seat on the piano bench. I'll be right there."

I looked around the room as I walked from the front door over to the black baby grand piano. All of the boxes had been unpacked and moved out of the room, and white lace curtains hung above the wood framed windows. I could see the side of my house through one of the windows as I looked over the top of the piano.

Beside her floral sofa, Miss Lucille had added a chair that was covered in shiny green material. There was a round wooden table on the other side of it. On the table she had a little statue of an angel sitting on a white doily. In the corner of the room was a tall, gold lamp with a white shade.

Mama said that our furniture was Early American and that Miss Lucille's house was Victorian. Our house had a lot of wooden paneling and tan carpet that Daddy had installed himself. Our furniture was mostly brown and was bought second hand. My room used to be our garage, so it was hot in the summertime and cold in the winter.

Miss Lucille's house was a lot more girly than our house. It was pretty obvious that she loved the color pink. On her pink sofa, she had pink pillows, and on her kitchen table was a vase full of pink silk flowers. A ceiling fan was spinning overhead, but the room was still hot. I sat on the piano bench and read the word "Baldwin" in gold letters on the front of the piano.

When she came into the front room from her bedroom, Miss Lucille was wearing yellow pedal pushers, a yellow short-sleeved knit top, white shoes with pointed toes and red lipstick. She held some papers against her body under her left arm as she was tying a bright green scarf in her hair.

She smiled and said, "It's so hard to find anything around here. I had to stop and try to remember where on earth I put my music supplies. It was all in there in the bedroom. What a silly place!"

She took both of my hands in her hands and said, "Nice long fingers. That's good. Let's start with the treble clef and the base clef, and then we'll go over the notes. We might even play some scales today. What do you think about that?" She was very happy.

I nodded okay. She smelled like roses and lilacs. "Is your piano a boy?" I asked.

She tilted her head to one side. "I don't think pianos are boys or girls. That's a funny question, Bobbi!" She laughed and patted my hand.

"It says Baldwin right here. That sounds like a boy." I pointed to the gold letters.

"So it does. That's the company that makes pianos. They make the very best. Baldwin is a good name for my piano. I like it. I want you and Baldwin to be good friends." She patted the piano just like she had patted my hand. "Let's get started."

Forty-five minutes went by fast, and then I was leaving her house with a pack of music flash cards to help me learn all of the music terms and notes plus some staff paper so I could practice drawing treble and base clefs. She told me that since I didn't have a piano at my house, I was welcome to practice at her house while she was teaching her classes at Bishop College. She showed me where she kept an extra key under the back door mat in case her door happened to be locked.

No one in our neighborhood ever locked their doors, and everyone slept with their windows open and their attic fans on unless they were lucky enough to have window units to cool off their bedrooms.

"See ya Thursday," I called as I ran down her front steps. I knew that Katie and Law were waiting for me at our fort. I dropped the flash cards and staff paper at my house, told Mama that my lesson was good, and I hurried to the back of Miss Lucille's yard.

Katie and Law had climbed onto the roof of the garage where Miss Lucille parked her car. The garage was closer to our fort than it was to her house.

"Hey," Law yelled. "Up here!"

"We're watchin' cars drive by. We saw you runnin' over to your house," said Katie.

I dashed around to the back of the building that was big enough for only one car. I quickly climbed the mimosa tree that grew beside it.

The three of us were lying on our stomachs on the shed roof when I spotted Miss Lucille opening the screen door at the back of her house.

"Scoot down," I whispered. "She's comin'."

She walked to her car, started the engine and backed her car out onto Bishop Street without seeing us.

"That was close," said Law.

"Sure was," added Katie. "Can you play the piano now?"

"I just started today." I was tickling my face with a mimosa leaf. "She told me that I have potential."

"What's potential?" Katie asked screwing up her face.

"It means I might be good if I practice a lot."

"Sounds like homework to me," said Law. "Where's she goin'?"

"Prob'ly the store."

"Meme said that she dresses like a floozy," said Law.

"She does not." I wasn't sure how a floozy dressed, but the way Law said it didn't sound nice. "When did she even see her?"

"Waterin' her yard. Meme said her clothes are too tight, and her shorts are too short."

"My mama told my daddy she better not catch him even lookin' this way," said Katie.

"Meme said she shouldn't be teachin' at the colored school. It's not right."

"What's wrong with it?" I turned on Law.

"Meme said that those colored boys will take advantage of her."

It was time to change the subject. "Let's play kickball." We climbed down from the roof and ran toward my backyard.

I was sure hoping that no colored boys would take advantage of my pretty piano teacher.

⚊⚊

Long, lazy summer days gave way to warm, humid evenings that were perfect for catching lightning bugs in jelly jars. Most nights after dinner my parents sat on our front porch with Mavis and Howard Baxter and talked about the news which was mainly about who would be our next president.

"Not sure what I think about the Democrats maybe pickin' a Catholic next month at the convention," said Daddy. "I sure don't want the Pope thinkin' he can be callin' our president and tellin' him what to do all the time."

"Don't feel good about it myself, but everybody at the plant is sure talkin' about that Kennedy fella," added Mr. Baxter who has dark brown hair and wears thick black glasses that make his eyes look even bigger than they are. He has a habit of hiking up his trousers because he wears his belt under his big belly. Katie said that he loves sweets. Mavis said that he loves donuts too much. He shuffles when he walks which was just the opposite of Daddy.

Daddy has more energy than anyone I know. He was a famous athlete in high school and keeps himself in good shape to set an example for his players. Mama says that he was one of the best athletes his high school had ever seen. He played football, baseball and basketball even though he is only five feet eight inches tall, and Mama says that might be stretching it. Mama is five feet two inches tall, and people at the church call them "a cute little couple." In the summertime Daddy does fancy dives off of the high diving board at the city swimming pool. That makes me proud.

"I think Jack Kennedy's real handsome, and that Jackie is mighty stylish," Mama told Mavis. "And I would love it if we had small children in the White House for a change."

"Should be quite a contest in the fall what with all the experience Nixon has had. I do like Ike, and I'm sure Nixon got good trainin' from him." Mavis is taller than Mama, but she's what Daddy calls a thick woman. She doesn't have much of a waist and has blonde frizzy hair that she pushes back from her face with a bando. She doesn't wear shorts even in the summer. Katie said that she has varicose veins from teaching all day and doesn't like to show her legs.

"Texas'll probably vote for the Democrats—Catholic or not," said Mr. Baxter.

"Not so sure about that. Nixon was Navy like me and took on those Commies, too. Nothin' timid about 'im," my daddy said with a nod. He looked around and asked no one in particular, "Where's that music comin' from?"

Everyone listened.

"Lucille's house," answered Mama. "She's havin' company tonight. Practicin' for a program at the school."

"They're sure makin' a lot of racket," said Mr. Baxter.

Daddy got up from his lawn chair and walked over to the corner of our house.

"Well, I'll be John Brown," he said as he turned toward the other adults. "There's colored folks in there with her."

"Where?" asked Mr. Baxter as he joined Daddy.

"Right there in her livin' room at the piano. They're cuttin' up and carryin' on to beat all," Daddy said.

"Jack, hush."

"Woman, you think they can hear me?"

"I told Mavis. It ain't right, what she's doin'."

"They're her students," said Mama. "I told you they're practicin' for a music program."

"Oughtta practice at the school then. Just stirrin' up trouble is what I think. Next thing you know coloreds'll be wantin' to buy a house right here in our neighborhood. Run our property values right into the ground," Mr. Baxter said pointing at the grass.

"She's lonely," said Mama. "She lost her husband. I feel sorry for her."

"Why can't she find some friends somewhere else?" Daddy asked.

"Maybe I'll invite her to church."

"Just tell her not to bring her colored friends," grumbled Mr. Baxter.

"Time to get ready for bed, kids," said Mama. She was frowning.

I turned to look at Miss Lucille's house. Through her window I could see she was playing her piano. Three colored boys and two colored girls were standing behind her. They were clapping and dancing as they sang. I could hear the words. It was a song we sang in music class at school.

"He's got my brothers and my sisters in His Hands,
He's got my brothers and my sisters in His Hands,
He's got my brothers and my sisters in His Hands,
He's got the whole world in His Hands."

"We best all be on the lookout for trouble from those coloreds. Some just like 'em are already causin' trouble in North Carolina and Nashville. Havin' those sit-ins like they think they can eat with white people," said Mr. Baxter. "Whoever wins the White House is gonna have his hands full, and that's a fact!"

When Mama came in to tell me goodnight, she started running her fingers through my long hair with both hands. She did that when she was nervous.

"Have you said your prayers, honey?"

"No, ma'am. I was about to."

I knelt beside my bed and folded my hands together. I could feel her standing next to me.

"Dear God, thank you for Mama and Daddy and Betsy and Katie and Law. Please help Mr. Baxter to not be so mean about Miss Lucille. Amen."

"Amen," echoed my mother. "Mr. Baxter doesn't know he's bein' mean. He was just brought up to think that white people and colored people should stay with their own kind."

"Why?"

"It's always been that way here, Bobbi."

"Essie Mae comes to Katie's house, and she's colored. She bakes sugar cookies and rocks Annie to sleep."

"I know, honey. She does the cleanin' and ironin' for them. That kind of thinkin' may not be right, but that's the way it is.

People just have their places. Essie Mae is their maid. You know Manuel mows our yard and helps your daddy when he needs things moved around here or at the field house, but he can't come to supper at our house. That would make people start talkin', and pretty soon your daddy would be lookin' for another job."

"Maybe she doesn't know about how things are in Marshall. Maybe you need to tell her."

"Maybe I do. Now you get some sleep, and don't worry your pretty little head about Miss Lucille." She kissed me on the cheek.

"Yes, ma'am." I shut my eyes.

⊷⊹ ⊹⊶

Mama visited Miss Lucille several times during the next couple of weeks. I kept on with my piano lessons and even went to her house to practice while she was teaching summer school at Bishop College.

One afternoon I was playing my scales, and I heard the screen on her back door creak. I stopped playing and listened. I heard a man's voice talking very low. Then I heard Miss Lucille answer him. She was laughing softly as she said, "No. No. You can't come in. One of my students is here. Get along now."

I heard the screen door shut, and she came into the front room.

"Those scales are improving. I heard you playing just now." She looked happy, and her cheeks matched her red lipstick.

"I'm gettin' faster," I told her.

"Why don't you try 'Heart and Soul' for me? I know you've been working on it. Be right back."

She left the room, and I could hear water running in her bathroom. I started playing the song the two of us sometimes played as a duet.

When she came back into the front room, her face was not as red.

"Do you have a boyfriend?" I asked her.

"What a question, child!"

"Mama says that you must be lonely. That's why you let colored people come to your house."

Her smile turned sad. "I work with colored people, Bobbi. They treat me nice, and I treat them nice. They're my friends. They're no different from you and me. Just their skin is a different color. Your mama's been a friend to me, too. I don't have many other friends here yet."

"I'm your friend," I told her.

"I know you are, and I thank you for that. Now you better be going on home. Your sweet mama will be wondering where you are, and I have a lesson to give here soon."

"Okay." Without thinking, I crossed the room, hugged her tight around the waist and then ran out the front door and down her front steps.

A boy taller and older than me carrying a music book and wearing a baseball cap was coming up her front walk. He was white. I was glad.

Just two nights after I heard Miss Lucille laughing with a man at her back door, loud screaming from next door woke me up in the middle of the night. Bright lights were flashing, and I could hear people talking right outside my bedroom window. The Van Worths were an older couple who lived in the red stone house next to ours. Their daughter, Lottie, was an old maid. She lived with them and taught Spanish at the high school. The loud noise woke Betsy, too. She started crying. Mama came into our room.

"Who's hollerin', Mama?" I asked with a sleepy voice.

"Your daddy's gone to check. Something happened next door. I think the police are here," she said as she patted Betsy's back hoping she would go back to sleep.

When Daddy came back in the house, I heard him tell Mama that Lottie had seen a man peeping in her window. She had gotten up to go to the bathroom. When she came back to her bedroom, there he was staring at her through the screen. She screamed and woke up her parents. They called the police.

"Not a sign of the Peepin' Tom now," Daddy told Mama.

"You better check all the screens and lock the doors." I could hear worry in Mama's voice.

"Go on back to bed. I'll check around and be there directly."

He tiptoed into our room trying not to wake Betsy. He checked the screen on my window. It was locked.

"Daddy," I whispered.

"What is it, Bobbi girl?"

"What did the Peepin' Tom look like?"

"Don't know. Lottie didn't get a good look at him. It was dark. She thinks he was wearin' a ball cap. She mainly saw his eyes. He ran away when she screamed."

"I'm scared, Daddy," I told him.

He sat down on my bed. "Baby, there's no need to be scared. He's long gone from here by now. Lottie screamin' like that prob'ly scared him more than he scared her. The police came. He won't be back around here, so you go on back to sleep now," he said and patted my head.

"Night, Daddy."

"Sleep tight, sweet girl."

I burrowed under my cotton sheet until only my eyes were showing. I was looking at the window hoping against hope that I wouldn't see any eyes staring back at me.

⚔⚔⚔

When the sun came through my curtains the next morning, I heard voices outside. I got dressed and went into the front yard where a man was talking to Daddy. He had a white moustache and was wearing a straw cowboy hat. He was smoking a skinny brown cigarette.

"Hey, Daddy," I said as I tugged on his left hand.

"Detective Binotti, this here is my daughter Bobbi. The detective is here about last night. He comes to all our games. I was just telling him about Johnny Dinkins. Quick as lightnin' outta the back field."

"You catch the Peepin' Tom?" I asked the detective.

"Not yet, little lady, but we're lookin' for him." He flicked his ashes toward the sidewalk.

"Why was he lookin' at Lottie? She's old," I said.

"Bobbi, that's enough. Better go in the house now and let the detective do his job."

"Okay." I was disappointed. "Hope you find him real quick-like."

"We'll do our best."

As I was walking slowly back to my house, I heard Daddy ask the detective if Lottie thought that the Peepin' Tom might be colored. I couldn't hear his answer.

Katie, Law and I spent most of the morning on Katie's front porch swing watching Detective Binotti walk from house to house. First he went inside the Van Worths' house, and then he came out and walked around their yard. Mr. Van Worth was stooped over, but he followed behind the detective who stopped by the window where Lottie had seen the Peepin' Tom. He stayed there for a long time looking at the ground and examining the screen.

Then he walked next door to the Sewells' house. Mr. Sewell was at work, but Mrs. Sewell came out on her front porch to talk to him. She shook her head no several times.

He crossed the street and knocked on the front door at the Tressells' house. When nobody came, I jumped out of the swing and ran over to tell him that Mr. Tressell worked the night shift at the railroad and that Mrs. Tressell was in a wheelchair. That was the reason there was a ramp leading up to their front porch.

"Maybe you should come back later. Mama said they're not mornin' people."

He smiled. "You know a lot about your neighbors, don't you?"

"Yessir. I've lived here most all my life."

"And just how old are you, young lady?"

"Ten. I'll be eleven on my next birthday in February. This is Katie. She's eight, and Law is ten like me." Katie and Law had joined me on the sidewalk in front of the Tressells' house.

"We've never had a Peepin' Tom before," said Katie. "What was he lookin' at?"

"Don't know for sure. Sometimes people just like to look at other people. I don't think he was goin' to hurt Miss Van Worth, so you kids don't need to worry."

"Lottie's old," said Law.

"So I've been told," he looked at me and smiled.

"Are your parents home?" he asked Katie and Law.

Katie responded, "My mama's home. She's a teacher, but she doesn't teach in the summer. We live upstairs there." She pointed at their apartment.

"What about downstairs? Who lives there?"

"Tada and Nona, my grandparents. Nona's home," Katie said. "Tada's at work downtown. He fixes jewelry."

"My grandmother's at home," said Law. "In that house there with the big magnolia trees."

"Thanks for your help. I'll be goin' to talk to them now."

We watched him walk away. He had on a stiff white shirt and khaki pants. I noticed that his left pant leg was caught up in one of his black cowboy boots. He was wearing a gun in a holster on his belt.

"That's a real gun," said Law.

"He might need it to shoot the Peepin' Tom," said Katie.

"I don't like that Peepin' Tom," I told them.

"Me either," said Katie.

"I wish I had me a real gun," said Law. "I would shoot that Peepin' Tom right in the eye."

I didn't think that Law would really shoot anyone, but I was pretty sure that other people in our neighborhood might.

JULY

July was hotter than June, and it didn't rain much. Katie, Law and I spent time in the shade building sand castles and filling make-believe moats with buckets of water from the water hose. Sometimes we accidentally on purpose sprayed each other with the water hose.

I practiced piano three or four times a week on Miss Lucille's piano. I tried to remember to curve my fingers and look at my music and not at my hands. Learning to play the piano was hard, but Miss Lucille bragged on me a lot. I did my best to please her.

Every July all of the neighbors met up in our backyard to celebrate July the 4th with a picnic. Daddy would cook barbecue chicken and corn on the cob on his outdoor cooker, and the women would bring cole slaw, potato salad, baked beans and deviled eggs. Katie's grandfather always brought a freezer of homemade ice cream to go with her grandmother's chocolate cake. Mr. Sewell insisted on bringing a watermelon because "it was not the Fourth without a melon."

I helped Daddy set up card tables and chairs for twenty-four people, and Mama showed me how to put her flag centerpieces on the red and white tablecloths. I thought that the backyard looked really pretty with crepe paper streamers and balloons hanging from every corner of our green fiberglass patio roof. Mama loved balloons better than anyone I knew.

"Happy Fourth!" Daddy called out to the Baxters who arrived first so that Mavis could help Mama in the kitchen with any last minute details. Katie and Annie had on matching blue and white short sets that Mavis made on her sewing machine. I was wearing red and white shorts with a blue ribbon tied around my ponytail. My aunt who lived over on the north side of town made most my clothes. She had embroidered my initials on the collar of my white blouse.

The Van Worths arrived next. They were in their late sixties which made them the oldest people at the party. Daddy said that when people were married for a long time, they started to look alike. I thought that was a funny thing to say, but maybe he was right. Both of the Van Worths had stooped shoulders, gray hair and pinched-in faces.

Their daughter Lottie was close to fifty, but she looked even older. She had pale skin and never wore any makeup. Not even any lipstick. She had pulled her long dark hair straight back from her face and fastened it with brown combs that she most likely purchased at Woolworth's. Her hair hung halfway down her back. She wore a brown dress with buttons down the front. I wondered if she had forgotten about wearing red, white and blue.

I was about to put Betsy in her playpen when Lottie walked across the yard and came right up beside me.

"Hello, Bobbi. Would it be okay if I held Betsy?" she asked. I was surprised because Lottie didn't have any children.

"Mama won't mind as long as you don't make her cry."

She sat down in a chair and started bouncing Betsy on her knee. Betsy started laughing.

As I sat down on the grass beside them, I said, "I didn't know you liked babies."

"I think babies are about the sweetest things in the whole world." She was talking baby talk to Betsy.

"She's not always sweet," I told her.

"Well, she's mighty sweet today."

"You ever wish you had gotten married so you could have some children?" I asked.

"I have lots of children. I have a whole new set of children each fall. I claim all of them as my own even though they don't realize it. I never got to bounce them on my knees, but each one is special to me."

"How many years have you been teachin'?"

"Twenty-eight. That's a lot of children," she laughed as she said it.

"Your knees would be worn out from bouncin' that many kids," I told her. "Why'd you pick Spanish to teach?"

"When I was a girl, I loved to read books about other countries. Spain was my very favorite place. I've always dreamed about going there. Maybe someday."

Before I could ask her to tell me about Spain, the Sewells arrived with a big watermelon. I had always been a little bit afraid of Sam Sewell because he was over six feet tall with black wavy hair and bushy eyebrows. He had a loud laugh that sounded just like a horse. Sandra Sewell was a tiny woman with deep set eyes and a little heart shaped mouth. The top of her head barely came up to Mr. Sewell's chin. Their only son was at summer school at the University of Texas in Austin.

Law, his stepfather Roy Ed and his mother Charla came through the gate into our backyard. Roy Ed was a round man with a shiny bald head. He was friendly and always had nice things to say to all of the ladies. I remembered that at last year's picnic he said I was pretty enough to be in the movies. I couldn't wait for Roy Ed to meet Miss Lucille since she looked like a real movie star. Charla Peteet was a grown up version of Law with the same dark hair and eyes, but she was lucky. She didn't have asthma. Charla was a teller at Marshall National Bank. Law bragged that she was very responsible with dollar bills and change.

"Hey," I said to Law as I met him near the fence. "You wanna ask Lottie about the Peepin' Tom?"

"She'll get mad," he said.

"She won't. She likes babies, and she's not as mean as she looks. I already talked to her about Spanish and other stuff."

We ambled over toward Lottie who had put Betsy back in her playpen and was sitting alone at one of the card tables.

"Miss Lottie, did the Peepin' Tom have bug eyes?" I asked. My question made her jump.

She raised both hands in front of her chest with her palms facing out towards me. I took a step back.

"Child, I declare, I don't know. It was so sudden seeing him like that looking right in my window at me." She shook her head from side to side.

"Bug eyes would be really scary. Like a monster," I told her.

"Was he colored, Miss Lottie?" asked Law. "Meme said she bet he was colored."

"I only saw his eyes. It was after midnight, you know. He could have been colored or white or red for all I know. His eyes were large and sinister looking," she said as she closed her own eyes remembering. "I'm still tossing and turning in my sleep. Can't get those eyes out of my head."

"Bobbi, you and Law leave Lottie alone," called Mama. "Go help Mr. Tressell with his dish. Mr. Tressell was carrying a glass plate covered with tin foil. He was a tall man with a brown leather face and arms. He worked at the T and P Railroad, and he had a large vegetable garden behind his house. His short brown hair had

31

some gray near his ears, and his eyes were as blue as the sky. Mama told me that Mr. Tressell was the same age as Daddy— thirty-nine. I had never seen Mr. Tressell wearing anything except denim overalls and a white t-shirt. He wore that to the picnic.

I hurried over to him. "I'll take that to the table for you," I offered.

"Did Ruth not feel up to comin'?" Mama asked him.

"Not havin' a good day. Sliced up some of our tomatoes. Hope you can use 'em," he said. Mrs. Tressell never came to the picnics.

As Mr. Tressell was walking over to the cooker where the men were sampling the chicken, I saw Miss Lucille open the gate. I skipped over to meet her. She was wearing a white blouse with ruffles in the front and back. Her navy pedal pushers, the blue ribbon in her hair and her red sandals made her look very patriotic. Her wavy red hair hung down past her shoulders.

"What'd you bring?" I asked looking at the Tupperware container she was holding. Law and Katie ran up beside me.

"What kind of trouble are you three up to today?" She smiled at us. "In here are some sugar cookies with red and blue sprinkles on top."

"Yummy." I licked my lips. "We can put 'em on the table for you." She didn't seem to know what to do next, so I took her hand and led her over to a lawn chair next to Mrs. Sewell.

"This is my piano teacher," I said. "She lives on the corner."

Mrs. Sewell smiled and said, "Sandra Sewell. Pleased to meet you. I heard you moved into the Fowler place."

"Lucille Harris. Yes. I'm on the corner. I finally seem to be getting settled. I should have been round to meet everybody by now, but with my classes at the college and piano lessons in the afternoon, time has just gotten away from me."

"I think I'll get some iced tea. Parched throat," Mrs. Sewell patted her neck as she got up and moved toward the table. "Get you some?"

"No, thanks. I'll wait for dinner."

Lottie Van Worth came over to meet Miss Lucille. "I teach Spanish at the high school. I hear that you teach, too."

"Piano and voice. I have a lot of talented students. Makes my job easy."

"Oh, to be so lucky," said Lottie. "Most of my students don't see a need for Spanish. How is it teaching at Bishop? Do you feel out of place?"

"Not at all. Everyone's made me feel right at home. The other teachers and the young people, too. I feel very lucky to be there."

Lottie raised her eyebrows.

"My lands. How could you feel lucky? Everybody I know is talking about the white lady teaching at the colored college. I tell you it's caused quite a stir at good old MHS."

Mr. Sewell walked up as Lottie was talking.

"Hear you had quite a scare last week, Lottie," he said. "Have they caught that naughty fella yet?"

"No, Sam, they haven't. Still makes my skin crawl to think about it."

"Was he colored?" Mr. Sewell asked. "I figured he was being so close to Bishop and all."

Before Lottie could answer, Miss Lucille said, "I teach at Bishop. I can't imagine any of my students doing such a thing."

"No offense meant, ma'am. It's just the close proximity and all. I know how young boys are. If I were you, I'd keep my screens latched and my doors locked—being such a pretty lady and all."

Sam Sewell glanced down at Miss Lucille's ruffled blouse. I wasn't surprised he had noticed how pretty she was. All of the men at the picnic had looked at her when she arrived. Her figure reminded me of the girls in the Miss America pageant that we watched on television.

Even Mr. Baxter who had said mean things about Miss Lucille seemed to want to visit with her at the picnic.

"How's your teachin' at the colored school workin' out for you?" he asked.

"I'm enjoyin' my students."

"Whatta you think about that business at Woolworth's in North Carolina?" he asked her.

"You mean about those young men wanting to eat at the counter?"

"That's what I mean—those colored boys thinkin' they can sit down right beside the white fellas. We don't allow that here, so you best not be encouragin' any of those coloreds boys you teach to try it."

"I teach music, Mr. Baxter. I don't involve myself in politics, but things are changing in this country."

Daddy tapped a spoon on his tea glass to get everyone's attention. Then he said grace over the food, asked a special blessing on our military, and we all lined up to fill our plates and enjoy the picnic.

Mr. Tressell was sitting at a table by himself when I saw Miss Lucille ask if she could join him. He nodded. Katie and I took the other two seats at their table. Charla made Law sit at a table between her and Roy Ed. I think she missed living with Law.

Everyone at our table was quiet until Miss Lucille said, "I do believe, this is quite a feast. I had trouble getting everything on my plate. And these are the best tomatoes I've ever tasted. They taste like home grown."

"Home grown in my garden," Mr. Tressell said. "Garden's behind my house."

"I always said there's nothing better than home grown tomatoes. I'd love to have a garden of my own and be able to pick my own vegetables."

"Squash, potatoes, turnip greens. Grow 'em all."

"Does your wife like to cook?"

"Pretty hard for her to get around in the kitchen. She manages though."

"Do you like football?" I asked, wanting to be a part of the conversation.

"Never had much time for football. Worked in the fields as a boy. Work the night shift now at the railroad."

"Do you come from a family of farmers?" Miss Lucille asked.

"Yes, ma'am. Lived on a piece of land about an hour and a half north of here outside of Texarkana. Small tract. Decent crops. Mighty poor. Five of us children. All had chores to do."

"Does your family live around here?"

"Moved away. Different parts of Texas. All of 'em."

"Do they come to visit?"

"Not much since my wife got sick," he told Miss Lucille. "Have one niece who comes to visit ever so often."

"I have a brother in Houston. I'm hoping he and his wife will visit me."

"Like that hammock over by my house, don't you?" he looked at me and then at Katie.

We both nodded. "It's fun to swing really high," Katie said.

"Sometimes, Law pushes me too high, and I fall out," I added.

"Wife told me. Thought you got hurt."

"Tell her I was okay."

"Think she knows."

"She watches TV a lot," Katie said.

"Not much else for her to do."

"Is she bad sick?" I asked even though I knew Mama would tell me I was meddling in the Tressells' personal business.

"Muscles in her legs don't work right. Been ten years. Woke up one day. Couldn't walk anymore. Took her to different doctors over in Shreveport. Nobody could help her. Finally gave up. Just make the best of it."

"I'm sorry," said Lucille.

"Sorry, too," he said. "Be happy to show you my garden. If you like."

"Would you? I would love to see a real garden. In Dallas, we didn't have a yard big enough for a garden, but I have plenty of room here to plant one."

"Saturday afternoon late. Come over. Be in the garden then," he said.

After dessert Daddy passed out sparklers to everyone, and then he lit the end of each one. The tip of my sparkler started to burn and then it crackled and fizzed, and sparks flew in every direction. Katie, Law and I twirled the sparklers and turned in circles as fast as we could. I felt like a ballerina with a magic wand. The sky was clear, and the stars were bright in the sky. The men told stories about World War II. Daddy had been in the navy on a submarine. Some of the other men had been in the army, and Mr. Sewell had been a pilot in the air force. He enjoyed telling about the missions he flew over Japan.

Daddy said that in Texas we were proud people all the time, but on holidays, we were especially proud of our freedom and those who fought for it.

All of the neighbors were laughing and having a good time visiting except for Mr. Tressell. He was standing by himself over near our fence staring at something. I looked to see what it was. Miss Lucille was sitting on a blanket holding my little sister. He was watching them.

⟞⟝ ⟞⟝

The Saturday afternoon after the picnic, we were taking turns swinging in the canvas hammock that was attached to two mimosa trees in Katie's side yard when Law spotted Miss Lucille walking down the street toward us. She was wearing a sleeveless blue cotton blouse, black shorts and white tennis shoes.

"Her legs sure are long," Law said.

"That's because she has on short shorts," Katie told him.

"Let's see where she's goin'."

"Where ya goin'?" I asked her when we met her on the sidewalk in front of the Tressells' house.

"To see Mr. Tressell's garden. He invited me at the picnic. Remember?"

I nodded my head.

We followed her up the sloped wooden ramp that led to their front door. She knocked. When no one answered, she headed around to the back and opened the side gate that led into the garden. We went back to Katie's yard and watched them through the chain link fence that surrounded his garden.

"Hello there," Lucille called to Mr. Tressell who was on his hands and knees pulling weeds in the garden. "I took you up on your offer to see your garden. Hope I'm not intruding."

"Nope," he said. "Here it is."

"Your front yard is just beautiful, and what a huge garden!"

I could tell by watching that he liked her compliments.

"How do you get your plants and vegetables to grow like this? You must talk to them or something."

"Talk to plants? No ma'am. Don't believe I ever heard of doin' that. Just work hard. Tend to the ones that need tendin' to. Fertilize when it's time. Keep things watered and mowed. Just comes natural, I guess."

"Well, I'm certainly impressed. I wish my yard could be a showplace like yours. Maybe if I work at it. I would love to enter the beautification contest that I read about in the newspaper, but it'll take a lot of work to make my yard look good enough." She laughed. "Are you going to enter, Mr. Tressell?"

"No, ma'am."

"Well, you should. You could win that contest."

Mr. Tressell and Miss Lucille started walking up and down the rows of leafy green plants. We could hear her asking him questions about each one.

Katie, Law and I soon got bored watching them. As we turned away from the fence to head back to the hammock, I saw Mrs. Tressell sitting in her wheelchair behind the screen on her back porch.

"Hey, Mrs. Tressell," I called as I waved to her, but she didn't wave back. She had her eyes on the people who were discussing vegetables in the garden.

AUGUST

"It's Blubber Lips," Katie whispered to Law and me.

We all turned to look at the skinny young man who was walking by Katie's front porch. Katie and Law were sitting in the porch swing. I was perched on the wooden banister dangling my legs over the side.

"He's goin' to work. Just like every day," I said, noticing the brown leather brief case that he held under his left arm. His sandy blond hair was in a crew cut, and his white dress shirt was already clinging to his back between his shoulder blades. He had his black tie tucked into his left shirt pocket to keep it from swinging back and forth as he walked. By the time he entered the front door of the Hub Shoe Store in downtown Marshall, his pale cheeks would be bright red from the summer heat.

"He walks on his tip toes," Law said. "It's funny-lookin'." He tried to copy him by walking around the porch on his toes.

"You can't do it in tennis shoes," I told him. "I don't even know how he walks like that in church shoes."

"Daddy says he's a sissy," said Katie.

Every weekday in the summertime, the young man we called Blubber Lips walked by our houses in the morning and again in the afternoon. He never looked our way. We gave him his nickname because he had especially large lips, but we were careful never to say his nickname in front of our mothers or Law's grandmother. Mama reminded me at least once a week to follow the Golden Rule and treat others as I would like to be treated. I figured as long as we only whispered about Blubber Lips among ourselves, we were not being mean to him. He could be calling us names to his friends, and we'd never know, but Mama still wouldn't be happy about it. I didn't think that Katie's father followed the Golden Rule since I'd heard Mr. Baxter use bad words when he talked about colored people and sissies.

Last summer I'd asked Daddy why some men were sissies, and he told me that I didn't need to worry about that sort of thing. He said that I would find out soon enough that some questions didn't have easy answers.

"I'm really hot. Let's go to the fort," said Law.

"Let's go." I hopped off of the porch railing.

We ambled across the street and waved hello to Miss Lottie who was watering her front yard with a green water hose trying her best to keep the grass alive.

"Hey, Miss Lottie!" I called to her.

"Stay out of trouble," she called back as she sprayed water in our direction.

The shade from the mimosa tree and the dirt floor of our fort felt a little cooler in the August heat. In just a little over a month, school would be starting again. Mama said that we were all trying to survive "the dog days of summer." We didn't have a dog because Daddy said that we didn't need one more mouth to feed, but I knew that even dogs would be too hot to do anything but lie around in August in Marshall.

The Democratic and Republican party conventions had been on television the month before. Mama and Daddy had talked about them every night at the supper table. We had watched the speeches on television. Daddy said that it was good for me to watch and listen because as Americans, it was our duty to know all about who was running for president of our country.

John F. Kennedy and Lyndon B. Johnson, a Texan, were the Democratic candidates, and Richard Nixon and Henry Cabot Lodge were the Republicans. Daddy was sure that Texas would vote for Kennedy even though he was a Catholic. Texans always supported other Texans, and Daddy said that most of the people he talked to when he went to the post office liked LBJ. I thought he had really big ears.

Mr. Nixon had been serving our country as vice- president and had two daughters who were teenagers. Mr. Kennedy was a senator and had a young daughter, and his wife was expecting a baby. Walter Cronkite said on the television that this would be the first election that people in Hawaii and Alaska could vote for president. They were our newest states. He said that everyone expected the election to be very close.

At supper last night after our normal election talk, Daddy told Mama that he was worried about colored people causing problems in downtown. I listened real close to what he said. After two-a-day football practice that afternoon, one of the other coaches told him there was talk of a sit-in at the courthouse. Some colored boys in South Carolina had been upset because the white people in Woolworth's wouldn't serve them at the food counter. Now it sounded like college kids in other towns were doing the same thing. Daddy said that the talk was that some college kids in Marshall were planning to go to Woolworth's on the square right across from the courthouse. They were planning to try to order food there and eat with white people.

Mama said that she didn't envy the new president at all. He would have a hard job on his hands.

———

We were pretending to defend our fort from the enemy when we heard voices coming from Miss Lucille's backyard. We crawled silently on our bellies like soldiers in the movies. Mr. Tressell's pickup truck was blocking our view. It was parked right behind Miss Lucille's car in her garage.

We would have shimmied up the mimosa tree to the roof of the tiny garage, but the tin roof was too hot this time of year. Instead we peered around the back end of the truck—Law on top, me in the middle and Katie on the bottom—like a totem pole with dirty faces.

Miss Lucille was sitting on her back porch steps, and Mr. Tressell was leaning against the side of her house. Both of them were drinking something cool. I licked my lips. I was thirsty just watching them. She was smiling as she talked, and he was smiling as he listened.

"What's he doin' here?" whispered Law.

"Don't know," I whispered back.

"Maybe talkin' about vegetables some more," said Katie.

"I never saw him smile before," said Law.

Almost as if he had heard us talking, Mr. Tressell handed Miss Lucille his tea glass and started walking toward the side of the yard. He was pointing at a grassy spot that was covered with weeds.

We heard her call to him, "Would that be the best place?"

"Best place for what?" asked Katie.

I shrugged.

"Has good sun. Looks like good soil. Weeds are growin' good." Mr. Tressell knelt down and rubbed some dirt between his fingers.

"Then that will be my new garden," she exclaimed as she raised her tea glass in the air toward him. "What do we do first?"

"Too early to plant. Need to get the soil ready. Have a hoe?"

"In the garage in front of my car. I'll get it for you," she told him.

As she stood up from her porch steps, we moved quickly back into the woods.

She came out of the garage with an old, rusty hoe. As she lifted it in the air to show it to Mr. Tressell, the metal blade fell off. She was reaching to pick it up as Mr. Tressell came over beside her.

He knelt down, and they each put a hand on the blade. They seemed to freeze in that position. His hand was on top of her hand. She looked up at him and smiled. He smiled back at her.

It was like watching Marshal Dillon and Miss Kitty on "Gunsmoke." Mr. Tressell offered her his right hand. He helped her up and picked up the broken hoe.

"Fix this up for you. Won't help us much like this."

"Thank you, Jim. I would appreciate it," she said. "I guess you better be going." Her cheeks were red.

"Start tomorrow on your garden. Same time?" He put the broken hoe in the bed of his truck.

"I'll have the tea ready and my work clothes on."

I wasn't sure that Miss Lucille owned any work clothes. She always looked clean. Today she was wearing white shorts and white tennis shoes with a pink t-shirt and a bright blue scarf in her hair. Mr. Tressell was wearing denim overalls without a shirt. His arms were really tan, and he had big muscles. He climbed back in his truck and waved to her as he slowly backed out of her gravel driveway onto Bishop Street.

She walked toward her back door and went inside. Within just a few minutes we heard piano music.

⊷⊶

For the next two weeks, Mr. Tressell parked his car in Miss Lucille's backyard, and each morning they worked getting the dirt ready for her garden. Her summer school term had ended, so she didn't have to teach in the mornings. After they worked for a while in the heat, Miss Lucille would get red in the face and tell him that she was feeling faint from the heat. They would take a break from their hoeing and weeding and go inside her house to cool off.

We got bored waiting for them to come back outside, so we usually left the fort to play kickball or swing in the hammock.

One morning in mid-August I happened to mention to Mama that I thought that Miss Lucille and Mr. Tressell were best friends.

"What do you mean by that, Bobbi?"

"He comes to her house every mornin' to help her with the garden she wants to plant in the fall. They work and talk and then go in the house to cool off."

"Mmm," was all Mama said.

"Why'd you say, 'mmm,'?"

"Just seems a little curious to me, that's all."

"You said she needed to make some friends besides her colored friends at the college. I thought you'd be happy."

"I remember tellin' you that, all right. I was meanin' some other women friends, that's all."

"Maybe you should take her another pie."

"I'll think about it, but right now I have to fix your daddy's lunch, so you run along and play some more."

"Yes, ma'am."

I went outside and was walking back toward the fort to see if Katie and Law were there when I saw Mr. Tressell holding hands with Miss Lucille as they stood near his truck. She was staring up at him. I stopped and hid behind a pine tree and peeked around it. He kissed her on the lips. Why'd he do that? I didn't want to bother Mama again, so I just stood very still until Mr. Tressell finally climbed into his truck and drove away. Miss Lucille went back inside her house.

I walked slowly to her back door and knocked softly. She was at her kitchen sink washing some dishes and humming.

I knocked a little louder. That seemed to startle her. She turned her head toward the door.

"Oh, Bobbi. It's you."

"I knocked, but you didn't hear me."

"Come on in. Did you come to practice piano?" She was drying a green tea glass.

"Yes, ma'am, if it's okay. I was botherin' Mama while she was cookin'. I was tellin' her that you and Mr. Tressell are best friends."

She dropped the glass in the sink. It broke into several pieces.

"Oh. Look what I've done now." I watched as she picked up the broken glass and put each piece into a small white plastic trash can under the sink.

"You go ahead and practice. Let me get this cleaned up. I'll be in to check on you in a minute."

She seemed jumpy, so I hurried into the front room, said hello to Baldwin and started to play a very slow version of "Amazing Grace."

SEPTEMBER

August crawled into September with temperatures reaching close to 100 and humidity almost the same. I complained to Mama that I was very sweaty, and she told me that she read in Good Housekeeping magazine that "Southern girls don't sweat. They glisten." I told her that I was glistening every day before breakfast.

Labor Day officially ended summer, and school began. Katie, Law and I met on the sidewalk each day at 7:30 to walk to school together. We carried our book satchels and wore penny loafers as we headed towards Miss Lucille's house on the corner, turned left to pass by her garden and garage and then turned right after two more blocks onto Houston Street. Stephen F. Austin Elementary was just a couple of blocks from there. On sunny days we would take a short cut through colored town. It was a much shorter walk to our school, but the roads were dirt, so our penny loafers would get muddy if we walked that way on rainy days. Today was a sunny day, so we skipped past colored children about our same age heading in the opposite direction. I had asked Mama back when I was in third grade why those children didn't go to our school since it was so close to their houses, but she told me that colored children had their own schools.

This morning as we passed Miss Lucille's yard, we waved to her and Mr. Tressell. They were working in her garden. Some days we didn't see them, and I figured that she was probably glistening and needed to go inside to cool off. Mr. Tressell must have been keeping her company since his truck was almost always in her driveway at 7:30 on school mornings.

Mama decided that I could keep taking piano lessons on Monday afternoon each week even though I had homework now that I was in fifth grade. I had overheard her tell Mavis Baxter that I was really good at the piano. Miss Lucille let me practice at her house on Saturday and on Tuesday afternoon when she didn't teach private lessons.

Her fall classes at the college had started again, and three days a week she had piano students. Nobody took lessons from her on Friday because most people in Marshall planned their Friday nights around the Marshall Maverick games. Fall was an especially busy time for Daddy since he was the head coach of the Mavs. He had practice every afternoon, junior varsity games on Thursday and varsity games on Friday night. He was at the field house or out scouting other teams on Saturdays. We didn't see a lot of him during football season, but Mama and I were used to that. Daddy had a good feeling that the team would be in the running for the district title this year.

Everybody, including me, had pretty much forgotten about the Peepin' Tom until Mama took Betsy and me with her to Abraham's grocery store one day after school. Miss Beverly was checking our groceries and was asking Mama about the football team when I noticed our sacker's bug eyes. I squatted down low to get a better look since his head was almost inside the brown paper bag. He seem to notice me then and scowled. I jumped up and moved behind Mama so that he couldn't see me watching him.

After Mama paid Miss Beverly for our groceries, I was climbing in the front seat of our station wagon when the boy with bug eyes put our bags in the back. I heard him say in a low voice, "Shouldn't be starin' like that."

He must have startled Mama because she said, "Were you talkin' to me?"

"I don't like people starin' is all."

Mama glanced over at me in the front seat. I sat very still and looked straight ahead.

"I'm sorry if we were starin' at you. We'll mind our manners better next time."

He grunted and headed back across the parking lot.

After she turned the key in the ignition switch, Mama asked, "Could he have been talkin' about you, Bobbi?"

"Did you see his bug eyes? I bet he's the Peepin' Tom. Maybe Miss Lottie could come here and take a look at him from the eyes up. I just know she could tell for sure if she did!"

"Bobbi Ann, where in heaven's name did you get that kind of idea? He's a teenage boy sackin' groceries at Abraham's. I didn't even notice him."

"You were talkin'. That's why you didn't notice. I'm just sayin' they're bug eyes, and he's skinny, too."

"Well, a lot of teenagers have bug eyes and are skinny. That doesn't make him the Peepin' Tom. Let's get on home and not think about it anymore. It's not nice to stare at people. You need to remember that."

"Yes ma'am," I said, but I was already thinking about how to get the news about the Peepin' Tom to Detective Binotti.

⊷⊹⊱

The Mavericks won their first three games. Talk around town was all about winning district. Marshall people loved football. Grown men even came out to watch the practices, and the Booster Club meetings on Monday nights after each Friday night game were standing room only. I cut out every article from the *Marshall News Messenger* about the Mavericks. I was making a scrapbook for Daddy since he had a feeling that this was the year that the team might go all the way to state.

There were some headlines in the paper about the election for president which was still about two months away, but there wasn't any more news about colored boys having sit-ins anywhere.

Miss Lucille's garden was really starting to green up. At my piano lessons she would tell me which vegetables were ready to be picked. She seemed really proud of herself. I wasn't all that keen on vegetables, but I liked to hear her talk about her garden since it made her so happy.

"You and Mr. Tressell are both good teachers," I told her.

"How do you mean, Bobbi?" She seemed surprised.

"You teach me piano, and he teaches you about gardens and things."

"Hmm," was all she said.

"I mean, he must be good at teachin'. You smile a lot when you're in your garden with him."

"He's been very kind to me," she said.

"Does he ever wear a shirt?" I asked. "He always has on overalls. Daddy wears coachin' shorts most of the time, but he sometimes wears regular pants and shirts. Like when we go to church. Does Mr. Tressell go to church?"

"My, my, you are Little Miss Question today!"

"I wish you'd come to church with us. You'd especially like the music. I know you would. Our preacher tells good stories. Last Sunday he was preachin' about not lettin' a bird build a nest on your shoulder."

"A bird nest on a person's shoulder?" She asked as she opened a new piece of sheet music for me to play. "That sounds like a funny story."

"He said that if a bird lands on your shoulder, you have to be careful that he doesn't keep comin' back again and again. If you let the bird do that, he will build a nest and cause all kinds of problems for you. He said the bird's name is 'Temptation.'"

Miss Lucille seemed to catch her breath. When I looked at her face, I saw that her cheeks were red. I quit talking and started playing my music.

When my lesson was over, I gave Miss Lucille a hug and asked her if she was planning to come to the football game on Friday night.

"I have a program at my school," she answered as she shook her head no.

"Your school is busy all the time."

"Not all the time, but we do have recitals and choir performances that I have to attend since I'm one of the teachers."

"It doesn't seem right that they're on Friday night since everybody knows that the Mavericks play then."

"Well, we have our own events at Bishop, and I'm not sure that our students would be welcome at Maverick Stadium."

"I was just meanin' you could come. Seems like you're missin' out on a lot of fun."

"You don't need to worry about me, Bobbi. I'm having fun. I'm not sad anymore if that's what you're worried about. Now don't forget to study your flash cards."

"See you next time, Miss Lucille!" I headed home wondering what Miss Lucille was doing for fun.

⊷⊶

"Don't forget your jacket, Bobbi," Mama called to me as I opened the back door.

"I got it." I was hurrying to meet Katie. Mama had said that we could walk to the library in downtown Marshall to check out some books. The library was only half a mile from our house in a

50

two-story red brick building right across from Abraham's. I loved reading biographies and Nancy Drew books. Nancy was a girl detective. Katie knew that I wanted to be a detective when I grew up. Katie didn't want to be a detective. She wanted to be an artist, but she liked to read books, too.

We handed our library cards to Miss Vera at the desk when we were ready to check out our books, waved good-bye to her and then crossed Franklin Street to Abraham's. I wanted to show Katie the boy with bug eyes, but we didn't see him. He must've been inside sacking groceries. Then I saw it. There was a big sign that said "City Jail" on the building across the street from Abraham's on Houston Street.

"Let's go see Detective Binotti."

"Who's that?" Katie asked.

"He's the detective who came when the Peepin' Tom was lookin' in Miss Lottie's window. You remember him. I bet he's at the city jail. Right over there," I pointed that way.

"I don't know. I've never been to a jail."

"We won't see the bad people. We'll just see him. I have to tell him somethin' important."

Katie said okay, and we walked another two blocks and crossed the street. I pulled open the heavy door under the City Jail sign. There was a tall counter with a policeman standing behind it. Katie and I stood on our tiptoes so that he could see us.

"What can I do for you girls?" he asked us.

"We need to see Detective Binotti. He's a friend of my daddy's. I need to give him a message," I explained.

"And who might your daddy be?"

"Coach Rogers. He coaches the Mavericks."

"Well, I reckon' I know him. Quite a season the boys are havin'."

"Yessir. They may go all the way to state this year," I bragged.

"Wait right here. I'll see if Al's in his office," he said as he turned to walk down the hallway.

There were two wooden chairs backed against one of the dirty green walls, so we both sat down. We could hear a man talking on the telephone. When the voice stopped talking, the policeman who knew my daddy and Detective Binotti walked up to the desk.

"What brings you little ladies to see me?" Detective Binotti asked with a smile on his face and a cigarette in his right hand.

"We were at the library. We saw the jail."

"Bobbi thinks that she saw the Peepin' Tom at Abraham's."

"She did, did she?" He looked me in the eyes.

"He has bug eyes. I saw him sackin' groceries when I went with Mama. He's skinny, too."

"I think I've got me a young detective here, Joe," he said to the policeman at the desk.

"That's what I want to be when I grow up—like you and Nancy Drew."

"I don't know if I can compete with Nancy Drew. She solves all of her crimes. Not quite like that in real life. Just like the Peepin' Tom case. Not an easy one to solve since Miss Van Worth didn't really get a good look at the fella. A lot of people have bug eyes."

"That's what Mama said. But he acts all shifty-like, too."

"Well. I'll just mosey on over to Abraham's one day and take a look. How 'bout that?" he asked.

"Okay," I said. "I guess we better be goin' now. Mama'll wonder why it's takin' us so long to check out books," I said.

"Thanks for stoppin' by. Bobbi, isn't it?"

"Yessir. This is Katie. She's my best friend."

"I remember meeting Katie, and you had another friend that day—a boy."

"Law Miller. His grandmother won't let him walk to town."

"He has asthma," said Katie.

He nodded like he remembered about Law. "Well, then, so long you two."

"If you catch the Peepin' Tom, will you tell us?" I asked as he opened the door for us.

"You'll be the first ones I tell right after the Van Worths." He chuckled.

OCTOBER

I didn't hear anything from Detective Binotti. Katie, Law and I were looking forward to our Halloween carnival at school, and I was working on a scrapbook about John F. Kennedy and Richard Nixon since the election was "right around the corner" as Mama reminded me.

Miss Lucille had taken me up on my invitation to come to church. She came the Sunday before Halloween and sat on the back row. During the visitation time when everyone said hello to everyone else, Mama saw her and asked her to come sit on our pew with us. She looked really pretty in a navy blue church dress with a white lace collar. Her red hair was hanging loose on her shoulders. After the preacher gave the invitation, and we sang four verses of "Just As I Am," Mama told Miss Lucille that she was so happy to have her visit our church.

"Bobbi invited me to come." She smiled at me.

"We have Sunday School classes, too. You could meet more people that way. Would you like to meet our pastor? He's only been here a little over a year, but everybody seems to like him," Mama told her.

"I would like that."

The four of us headed in the direction of Brother Rutledge who was shaking hands with all of the church members at the back of the church. He had wavy silver hair, a kind smile and soft hands.

"Brother Rutledge, this is our neighbor, Lucille Harris. This is her first time to visit," Mama told him.

"Well, now, we are mighty glad to have you worship with us today. What brought you to our fine town?" he asked her in his deep voice.

"I'm a music teacher—private lessons and at Bishop College."

He didn't act surprised that she was teaching at Bishop. He just smiled and took her right hand in both of his.

"We always have a place for musically inclined people here at the church. Singin' in the choir, leadin' a choir or playin' the piano—always a spot available, but you're welcome even if you don't want to be part of the music," he told her.

"That's good to hear."

"Tell Jack we missed him today, Nita."

"I will Brother Rutledge. He had to be at the field house this morning. I don't like him to miss church, but he had something come up with one of the other coaches. I'm sure everything will be okay," Mama told him as we walked out the door and down the front steps of the church.

"You wanna walk home with us, Miss Lucille? We walk on Sunday unless it's rainin'. Daddy says that saves on gas."

"I drove my car since I wore these high heels, but I'd love to give y'all a ride home."

"That would be so nice," said Mama. "Betsy's gettin' pretty heavy on my hip these days, and lettin' her walk by herself takes us forever. Jack usually puts her on his shoulders. I'll just get Betsy from the nursery."

"I'm right across the street. I'll wait for you there."

Mama put Betsy in the back seat next to me, and she sat in front with Miss Lucille. "I hope you won't think that Brother Rutledge was bein' pushy—tellin' you about needin' people who can sing. We do need a choir leader for our children's choir, but you need to make sure you like the church first. You never have to wait long before they start askin' you to serve."

"I'm in the children's choir," I said as I leaned my head over the front seat between them. "Our teacher had a baby and had to quit."

"I see," she said as she pulled up in front of our house.

"Bobbi tells me that you have quite a garden now. I'd love to see it some time."

"It must be beginner's luck. I have kale and cabbage and beans and even some tomatoes. I'd be happy to share some with you if you'd like."

"Well, that's quite a list. I think you have a green thumb," Mama said.

"Mr. Tressell's a good gardenin' teacher, isn't he, Miss Lucille?"

"Yes, he is. He's been a big help to me with my garden." Her cheeks were turning pink.

"We don't know the Tressells very well since Mrs. Tressell doesn't socialize. I'm glad he's been a help to you."

"Hmm," she said quietly.

When she didn't say anything else, Mama opened her car door.

"Bobbi's making good progress with her piano. She's my most conscientious student."

"I'm glad to hear that." Mama and I both smiled. "Time to feed these girls some lunch. Thank so much for the ride home, Lucille."

When we were in our kitchen, I asked Mama if she was planning to go see Miss Lucille's garden. I told her that Miss Lucille seemed to get all red in the face when I talked to her about Mr. Tressell helping her.

"I noticed her cheeks turnin' pink today, but she is a redhead and has such fair skin. I'm sure that Mr. Tressell just helped her get her garden started. He certainly has a big garden at his house to tend to."

"He helps her every mornin'. We see them on our way to school. One time I even saw him kiss her."

"Hush, Bobbi. He's a married man."

"He kissed her, and she put her arms around his neck, and she was all happy."

"When did this happen?"

"In the summer before school started. I knew I'd just be botherin' you if I told you."

"Well, let's not worry about it now. Maybe she was just thankin' him for his help. It was probably just that one time," she said. Mama never liked to think bad about anyone. "Time to eat our lunch now, so you can finish up your scrapbook for school. The election's next week."

As I glued pictures and articles in my scrapbook, I thought about how happy John F. Kennedy and his wife Jackie looked. She was always smiling at him in the pictures. I also wondered if helping Miss Lucille with her garden made Mr. Tressell happy. When we were swinging in Katie's hammock next to the Tressells' house, we could see Mrs. Tressell rolling around her kitchen in her wheelchair. She watched a lot of game shows on television, but we never saw her out in their garden or even out on their front porch. She had a sad face. Maybe Mr. Tressell just needed some happy times to push back against the sad times.

I was dressed like a football player for Halloween in shoulder pads, a helmet and the smallest Maverick jersey that Daddy could find at the field house. The jersey fit me more like a dress. Katie was dressed like Cinderella, and Law was dressed as a cowboy even though he didn't have any cowboy boots. He did have a white hat, a toy gun and a holster. We went to every house on Rusk Street trick or treating. When Miss Lottie came to her door and gave us each a Tootsie Roll, I asked her if she had heard any news about the Peepin' Tom. She said no, so I thought I better not mention the boy with bug eyes at Abraham's.

"I hope I never lay eyes on him again. I start shaking just thinking about it."

We stopped at the Sewells' house and then crossed the street to go to the Tressells' when Law said, "I don't think we should go there."

"Why not?" I asked him.

"I don't think they like Halloween. They didn't come to the door last year."

"Won't hurt to try again," I said as I ran up the ramp to their front door.

I knocked on the door, and nobody came.

"See," Law said. "They won't even come to the door."

Right then Mr. Tressell opened the door, and we said, "Trick or treat!"

"Forgot all about it bein' Halloween."

"Who's there?" Mrs. Tressell called from another room.

"Neighborhood children. Trick or treatin'."

"We ain't got nothin' for 'em," she said. "Tell 'em to go on."

"Justa minute," he said as he closed the door. I looked at Katie and Law. We didn't know what to do. We had decided to leave when he opened the door again.

"Here. Take these." He gave us each a tomato, and he closed the door.

"I never got a tomato for Halloween before," said Katie.

"Me either. I guess that's all he had."

"Why's Mrs. Tressell so mean?" asked Law.

"Don't know," I shrugged. "Let's get goin'."

We got hard candy from the Baxters and apples from Mrs. Lawrence before crossing the street to Miss Lucille's house. This was her first time to pass out Halloween candy. She heard us knocking and opened the screen door for us. She was all dressed up like Little Red Riding Hood. She told us that she had been baking caramel popcorn balls all afternoon and had wrapped them in wax paper so they wouldn't stick to everything. She invited us to come in while she went to her kitchen to get the treats for us. We were sitting on her sofa when we heard some people talking on her porch. Then someone knocked on the door frame.

"There's more people knockin' at your door," I called out to her.

"Tell them I'll be right there, Bobbi."

I walked over to the front door and looked through the screen. There were three colored boys standing there holding paper sacks. When they saw me, one of them said, "Trick or treat! We're here to see Mrs. Harris. She told us she was makin' somethin' special for Halloween."

"She's in the kitchen gettin' us some popcorn balls." I didn't know if she would want them to come in the house or not, so I just stood there staring at them.

"You her daughter?" asked the tallest one.

"No. I'm too old to be her daughter."

"Whatcha doin' in her house?" The shorter boy spoke this time.

"She's my piano teacher. We're trick or treatin'."

"She teaches us over at the college." The taller one spoke again.

Miss Lucille came to my rescue then. She called the boys by their names and opened the screen door to give them popcorn balls. They put them in their sacks.

The boy who hadn't said anything yet thanked her, and then said, "You goin' trick or treatin', too?"

"Oh, no. I just thought it would be fun to dress up. I'm Little Red Riding Hood."

"You better look out for big bad wolves," the tall boy said, teasing her.

"I don't plan on seeing any wolves tonight. Happy Halloween to you boys."

As they turned around, I heard the shorter one say to his friends, "She's lookin' mighty fine tonight. Yessir. Mighty fine."

Miss Lucille didn't seem to hear what he said. Instead, she turned to give each of us a popcorn ball from the glass tray she was holding. She brought us some lemonade, too, so we tore off the wax paper and ate our treats.

"Thanks for the popcorn ball. It was yummy," I told her. Katie and Law thanked her, too. "We better be goin' since it's gettin' dark."

"Thanks for sharing my first Halloween on Rusk Street with me. Tell your mothers and your grandmother hello for me."

As we were leaving her house, I saw the three colored boys sitting on the curb across the street from her house. They were eating their popcorn balls.

"Better watch out for goblins!" one of them hollered. We took off running. All three of them laughed.

NOVEMBER

The first Catholic president in the history of our country was elected in November which meant that LBJ would be vice president. Daddy said that Texans would be happy at least for a while.

"Why for just a while, Daddy?" I asked him.

"It's hard for politicians to please people for very long, Bobbi girl. Somethin' seems to crop up that causes some folks to become disgruntled with our elected officials. Sometimes they deserve it, and sometimes they don't. It can't hurt us that LBJ was on the ticket. It never hurts to have a good ole' boy from Texas close to the main seat of power."

"What made Mr. Kennedy win?" I asked him.

"I think a couple of things beat Nixon. He got hurt when he was campaignin' and then got an infection. He lost some weight after that and looked pretty bad."

"How'd he get hurt?"

"He banged his knee on a car door. Bad luck. Then in September in the first debate, remember we watched that one, he was just getting' over the flu and still runnin' fever."

"I remember he looked really sweaty."

"He didn't look good and didn't look straight at the camera the way JFK did. Nixon's a smart fella, but he always looks like he needs a shave, and he has pale skin. People compared him to Kennedy who had been out in the sun and looked healthy. Nixon just didn't seem to impress people in that first debate, and as you've heard your mother say over and over again, women just love Jackie, what with her pretty clothes and silly stuff like her furniture."

I nodded. "Mama likes readin' about her clothes and the parties she goes to."

"The election was really close. The most people in history voted, but in the end, I think that debate just stuck in people's minds and made all the difference."

"Just between you and me, are we gonna beat the Tigers and win district?" I had heard enough about the election and wanted to know if Daddy really thought we might be state champions.

"The Tigers will be our toughest opponents yet—even tougher than the Lobos, and they always give us a good game. I'm hopin' we can pull it out, but it'll be a close one, for sure. Don't you be tellin' anybody I said that. I don't want anyone thinkin' that I have any doubts about my boys. I just know how big and fast these guys we're goin' up against are. Maybe we'll be a little bit faster. I just won't know 'til we get our hands on the ball that night and line up against 'em."

"No turnovers. Right, Daddy?"

"That'll be the key."

Daddy was right. The Tigers were bigger and faster. Our Mavs played with a lot of class, but our season ended when the Tigers beat us 21-14 to become district champions. The state championship would have to wait until next year for MHS. With ten seniors returning, chatter about our chances would start again with the spring practice games. Until then we would have Daddy at home more often.

The Thanksgiving holidays were coming up. I loved turkey and dressing and cranberry sauce, but my favorite part of Thanksgiving was watching the college football games on television with Daddy. We would choose our teams and then see who had the most wins at the end of the day. As Baptists we didn't believe in gambling, so we didn't make any money bets. The winner got to have a cold Coca Cola which was a big treat at our house. Daddy usually won since he knew more about football than anybody, but I was hoping my teams might come through for me this year.

I asked Mama if Miss Lucille could come to Thanksgiving dinner at our house. She told me that she had invited her, but she was taking the bus to Houston to visit her brother. I was happy she had someone to visit with on the holiday. I knew that her birthday was the Monday after Thanksgiving. I had made her a special pot holder with my weaving kit. Since I was in her house so often, I knew her kitchen colors. I also knew that she could really use a new pot holder.

"Come on in, Bobbi," she called to me. "Why don't you practice your scales? I'll be right there. I have to make a quick telephone call."

As I sat down at the piano and started to play, a black car with a rainbow painted on the driver's door pulled up to the curb in front of her house. A man got out carrying a tall glass vase full of yellow roses. I hurried to the front door and opened the screen before he could even knock since I knew that Miss Lucille was talking on the telephone and couldn't come to the door.

"Hello there, little missy," the tall fellow with the fat belly said to me. "I have a delivery for Lucille Harris. She at home?"

"Yessir. She's here, but she's talkin' on the telephone. You wanna bring those flowers in here?"

"I do. I think they're too heavy for a little girl like you to carry. Where should I put 'em?"

"On the kitchen table over there," I said as I pointed the way for him. "Those are mighty pretty yellow roses. Who're they from?"

"I guess I better let the person who got 'em tell you that. I just deliver the flowers. I don't share any secrets," he said and winked at me.

I wasn't sure why he winked or what he meant by secrets, but I gave him a smile and put a white doily on the table so that the glass vase wouldn't make a ring. I counted the roses. There were twelve.

He sat them down making sure not to spill any of the water.

"Make sure she sees 'em directly," he told me. "I can show myself out the door."

"I will." I couldn't wait to see who they were from. Maybe they were for her birthday. I had my pot holder in my pocket to give her. It seemed pretty small compared to the flowers, but I was happy that she would have at least two gifts.

I was staring at the card that was lying on the table next to the vase of roses when Miss Lucille came into the kitchen from her bedroom.

"Where did those gorgeous roses come from?" she asked.

"A man brought them while you were on the telephone. I told him to put them here. I hope that was okay. He wouldn't tell me who they were from. I bet they're for your birthday. I made you a pot holder for your kitchen," I said as I handed her my gift, "so now you have two birthday gifts."

"Thank you, Bobbi. That's so thoughtful. I wasn't expecting anything for my birthday. My brother and his wife had a cake for me over Thanksgiving, but your gift and these roses really make it a special day."

"Aren't you gonna open the card? Who do you think could've sent you roses?"

"I don't have a clue, but let's find out." She had a big smile on her face as she picked up the envelope and opened it so that she could read the card inside.

"It says 'Happy Birthday from a Secret Admirer'." She looked on the back side of the card for a name, but there wasn't any other writing.

"Why wouldn't they want you to know who it was? I sure would. Roses cost a lot of money."

"I guess he wants it to be a secret." She was still smiling.

"Do you have any guesses?"

"Oh, I don't want to guess. It's more fun that it's a secret."

"Are you sure it's a man?"

"I would think so. I've never heard of a woman calling herself a secret admirer of another woman."

"Should I ask Mama what she thinks?"

"There's no need for that. Maybe my secret admirer will tell me soon enough."

"I couldn't stand not knowin'. I don't really like secrets very much."

"If you get beautiful yellow roses on your birthday, a secret's certainly worth having and keeping."

"Will you tell me who sent the roses if you find out?"

"I will if you can keep it a secret."

"Cross my heart and hope to die."

"Let's get to that piano lesson now. We're wasting your daddy's money by talking about yellow roses and secrets."

I sat down at the piano and started to warm up my fingers with my scales. She kept smiling, so I knew that she must be thinking about her secret admirer and the yellow roses.

⊷⊱ ⊰⊶

The Sunday after her birthday, Miss Lucille joined First Baptist Church. While everyone was singing "Have Thine Own Way," she walked down the aisle and shook hands with Brother Rutledge. We voted her in as a member of the church since she was moving her membership from another Baptist church and had already been baptized.

Sure enough right out of the box, Brother Rutledge asked her to lead the children's choir, so she started spending Wednesday evenings and Sunday evenings at the church. She never did tell me who sent her roses, but I was wondering if it might have been the youth minister at our church because he asked her to go to a movie at the Paramount Theater with him. I had seen them talking at Sunday night fellowships.

"I think Brother Billy has a crush on you." She was sweeping her front porch while I was hopping up and down her two porch steps.

"It's just a date to a see a movie, Bobbi."

"I bet he's the one who sent you the yellow roses."

"I don't think so. Not on a youth minister's salary, and besides, we're just getting to know each other."

"Have you been out on dates with other fellas?"

Her cheeks turned pink. "No. Not really."

"But somebody's got to be the secret admirer. Somebody likes you a whole, whole lot because roses are real expensive."

"I know they are, but I still don't know who sent them."

"What about somebody from your school or maybe even Mr. Tressell."

She stopped sweeping and stared at me.

"Why'd you say Mr. Tressell?"

"He could be your secret admirer. I know that he used to come to your house a lot to help you with your garden, and you seem to like him a lot."

"What makes you think I like him a lot?"

I didn't want to make her mad, but Mama said to always tell the truth, so I said, "I saw you kissin' him one time by his truck."

She dropped the broom and sat down on her porch swing. Then she covered her face with her apron.

"What's wrong? Mama said you're just friends with Mr. Tressell."

"You told your mother you saw us kissing?" Her cheeks were bright red when she lowered the apron.

I nodded my head.

"What'd she say?"

"She said you were just being polite and thankin' him for helpin' you with your garden. I bet that's why he sent you roses to thank you back for bein' so nice to him."

"You don't know who sent me the roses, so let's not talk about it anymore."

That was all she said before she got up from the swing, opened her screen door and went inside. I was really sorry I had brought up Mr. Tressell. Since she had asked me not to tell anyone about the roses, I couldn't even ask Mama if what I said was wrong.

Maybe she would like going to a movie with Brother Billy. He was closer to her age than Mr. Tressell, and he seemed to get along with grownups and teenagers at the church. Daddy thought he was silly, but Mama said that youth ministers had to be silly so that teenagers would like being around them. Miss Lucille didn't act very silly to me.

DECEMBER

The Christmas holidays were my very favorite time of year. Mama made hot chocolate and sugar cookies. Katie, Law and I decorated the cookies with icing although we ate more than we decorated. We were all in the children's choir at the church, so we had been practicing every Sunday night and every Wednesday night for the last three weeks for our Christmas program. Katie was singing a solo in the program, and I was playing "What Child is This" on the piano. Law was dressing up as one of the three wise men for the nativity scene.

The program was the Sunday night before Christmas. Mama dropped me off early in case Miss Lucille needed any help. We were expecting a full sanctuary of people. I was wearing my red Christmas dress which had lace on the sleeves. I had a green ribbon tied on my ponytail and black, shiny shoes and white Sunday socks on my feet.

When I came into the choir room, I saw Miss Lucille talking to Brother Billy over by the piano. Miss Lucille was wearing a bright green dress and red high heels. She looked as pretty as she had the day I saw her moving into her house, but she also looked sad. She was wiping her eyes with a handkerchief. This was a bad thing to happen right before the Christmas program. Brother Billy was patting her left hand.

"Hey, Miss Lucille. Hey, Brother Billy," I called out to them so they would know I was in the room.

Miss Lucille turned her head towards me and gave a little wave. Brother Billy said, "Hey there, Bobbi. Ready for the program?"

"Yessir. I'm ready. Mama dropped me off early in case Miss Lucille needed help with anything."

"That was very kind of her," he said.

"Are you all right?" I looked at her face. Her eye makeup looked runny.

She nodded but continued to wipe her eyes.

"Why don't you make sure that the printed programs are by both doors of the sanctuary, Bobbi," Brother Billy suggested.

"Okay." I backed out of the room. I stood by the door for a minute to see if she might come out into the hallway, but I could still hear the two of them whispering.

When I came back from checking on the programs, they were both gone.

As the other kids started to arrive, she came back into the choir room. She must have fixed her makeup because she looked pretty again and was doing her very best to smile at all of us.

The program was a big success, and the fellowship afterwards in the church parlor was even better. We all drank punch and ate Christmas cookies while the grownups told us what a good job we had done.

Everyone was complimenting Miss Lucille on the program which seemed to make her happy. I didn't see Brother Billy at the fellowship, but over in the corner by the piano I saw Mr. Tressell. I had never seen him at our church, but before I could make my way over through all of the people to say hi to him, I saw that the chair was empty. He was gone.

I waited until Miss Lucille was drinking some punch and eating a cookie before I walked up to her.

"Everybody sure liked the program tonight. I hope we made you proud."

"Of course, you made me proud. You always make me proud, Bobbi. Your piano special was one of my very favorite parts of the program," she told me.

I smiled up at her.

"Thank you. I'm glad you're not sad anymore. When you were cryin' before the program, I was afraid someone had been mean to you."

"Nobody was mean. I had to make a hard decision today, and it was hard for me to talk about it."

"Are you mad at Brother Billy?"

"Oh, no. I like Brother Billy. We're good friends. I'm just not ready to be more than that. He didn't want to hear me say it. It was hard for me to tell him. That's what made me sad."

"Did you see Mr. Tressell at the program? He was over there in the corner, but he left before I could say hi to him."

"Jim was here? I didn't see him." She looked around the room.

"I know it was him. I bet he came to see the program since you were leadin' it."

She patted my shoulder. "I will have to thank him for coming the next time I see him."

"He doesn't come 'round to your house anymore, does he? Is that because it's not gardenin' time?"

"Partly that, but partly it's because of something you said to me. You remember that day at your piano lesson when you told me about Brother Rutledge's sermon about not letting a bird build a nest on your shoulder?"

I shook my head. I remembered that Brother Rutledge had talked about a bird nest and temptation, but I didn't know what that had to do with Mr. Tressell and her garden.

"I knew then that I needed to change some things. I was lonely and made some mistakes. I needed to stop the bird from building his nest."

Mama and Daddy walked up then and said that we needed to head on home. It was Betsy's bedtime. I hugged Miss Lucille good-bye.

"Everything'll be all right," I whispered. She smiled down at me.

JANUARY 1961

Christmas vacation had come and gone. Santa brought me an electric football game. I loved to watch the little plastic players vibrate up and down the field. Law liked to play, too, but Katie got bored when the players got stuck on the sidelines or turned the wrong direction.

It was really cold outside in Marshall, so Katie and Law came over each day after school to play board games. On Friday, January 20th it was even colder in Washington, D. C. where John F. Kennedy was inaugurated as the 35th President of the United States. It was 20 degrees and had snowed there the day before which created quite a mess for people attending the ceremony. The Boy Scouts had to help clear snow from the streets for the parade. Mama watched the entire inauguration on television and told me that President Kennedy looked really handsome and that Jackie looked beautiful. We had a black–and–white television, but it was the first time that the inauguration was on television in color. We watched the evening news that night and heard David Brinkley describe the event and share some of President Kennedy's speech:

"And so, my fellow Americans: ask not what your country can do for you; ask what you can do for your country."

The next morning Marshall had snow which was great because it was a Saturday, and we could make a snowman. I put on gloves, a red wool cap, my black galoshes and my blue car coat and hurried across the street to call for Katie and Law. When they finally appeared, I suggested that we build a snowman in Katie's front yard. We all started to roll the snow into balls. Law's was the biggest, so his snowball became the bottom. We sat my snowball on top of his and then placed Katie's on top of mine. Now all we needed was everything to dress our snowman and make his face look good. We ran to my house to ask Mama for her help. She gave us a carrot from the refrigerator for his nose and some prunes to use for his mouth. She also loaned us a scarf to put around his neck. Law found two sticks to use for his arms, and Katie picked up some rocks to use for his eyes. We didn't have a top hat, so I took off my wool cap, and we sat it on top of his head.

Mama brought Betsy outside to see the snowman. She was carrying my sister on her right hip and our Brownie camera in her left hand.

"He looks great. What's his name?"

"Buster," said Law. "His name's Buster."

"Where'd you get a name like that?" I asked him.

"He just looks like somebody named Buster would look."

"Let me take your picture with Buster then," Mama said.

She handed Betsy to me. We stood on one side of Buster, and Katie and Law stood on the other side of him. Betsy grabbed hold of one of Buster's stick arms.

"That's so cute! I heard on KMHT this morning that we can send pictures of snowmen to the *News Messenger* to be part of a contest," said Mama.

"What's the prize?" I asked.

"Twenty-five dollars, and they'll put your picture in the paper."

"Twenty-five dollars is a lot of money!" Katie's eyes were big.

"You'd have to divide it three ways since you all worked on the snowman."

"That's still more money than I have in my piggy bank," said Katie.

"Me, too," added Law.

"I sure hope we win!" I said. "Just think what we could buy with eight whole dollars!"

"You should prob'ly save some of it and not spend it all at once," said Mama.

"Thanks for taking our picture, Miss Nita," Law said.

"When will we know if we win?" asked Katie.

"I'm guessin' not for a couple of weeks since people have to get their pictures developed and then drop them off at the newspaper office.

⚓⚓

We didn't win the snowman contest. Some college kids from ETBC built a really big snowman. He was over 10 feet tall. They put an ETBC flag in one of his arms and a blue and gold beanie on his head. They named him "Mr. ETBC Spirit." He looked better than Buster.

FEBRUARY

I turned my attention to Valentine's Day. My fifth grade teacher was named Mrs. Gerlach. She was very tall with black and gray hair that she combed into tight curls around her face. She loved pink lipstick and large gold earrings. She also loved Valentine's and wanted everyone in the class to decorate a box for our school party. I decided to make a rocket ship since President Kennedy had said that he was interested in sending men into space. I also liked watching "Pathfinders in Space" on television and learning about stars and planets in science class. I spent a couple of hours each evening cutting and pasting red, white and blue construction paper onto an old shoebox. I was good at cutting out letters, so when I pasted white letters that spelled USA on the rocket ship, it looked ready to fly.

On Valentine's Day everyone in my class brought their boxes to school. I had valentines to put in every box. Mama said that it was the right thing to do, but I noticed that some of my classmates didn't feel that way. They skipped Eddie Joe Wise's plain shoe box when it was their turn to pass out their valentines. Eddie Joe was bigger than all of the other kids in our class. He didn't smell good and had greasy hair. During class he would rub his hands up and down on his dirty trousers, and his tennis shoes looked too small for his long feet. Sometimes he even went to sleep during arithmetic.

I asked Mama why Eddie Joe didn't take a bath every night like I had to, and she said that not everyone had a bathroom and a bathtub like we had. She told me that Eddie Joe's family was really poor and probably didn't have running water in their house. Baths were much harder to come by for some people. I felt sorry for Eddie Joe, so when it was my time to put valentines in the boxes, I put two in his box. I hoped that would make up for the people who hadn't been nice to him. When it was his time to pass out valentines, he just looked down at the floor until Mrs. Gerlach called out to him.

"Eddie Joe, come to the front of the room. Your daddy must have left your valentines on my desk. There was an envelope with your name on it when I got here this morning."

Eddie Joe looked surprised and a little embarrassed when he had to walk to the front of the room. He opened the white envelope and smiled really big at Mrs. Gerlach when he saw all of the valentines inside.

"Go on now, Eddie Joe, and pass out your valentines."

He went from box to box and put an envelope in each one. He had one valentine left over, and he gave it to Mrs. Gerlach.

"Why, thank you, Eddie Joe. That's very thoughtful. Let's have cookies and punch, class, to celebrate this special day."

❦

A couple of weeks after the Valentine's party, Eddie Joe had a seizure in front of the class. He had been at the black board trying to add some numbers when he started shaking and fell on the floor. At first we all thought he was just trying to get out of doing his work, but when he kept shaking, we started screaming for Mrs. Gerlach to do something. His arms and legs were hitting the floor and the wall beside him.

Mrs. Gerlach asked Law to get Mr. Stinson, our principal, and then she hurried to the front of the room.

"Class, screaming will not help Eddie Joe. Praying will, so sit down, put your heads on your desks and pray that he will be all right." She put his head in the crook of her left arm and then put her wooden ruler in his mouth. His legs and arms continued to thrash around.

When Mr. Stinson came running into the room, he saw Mrs. Gerlach on the floor with Eddie Joe.

"How can I help?"

"Grab hold of his legs to keep him from hurting himself."

"A seizure?"

She nodded.

"I'm doing my best to keep him from swallowing his tongue. It should be over soon."

The school nurse, Miss Amanda, came into the room. Law was right behind her.

"Let me take over for you," she told Mrs. Gerlach. She knelt beside them.

"I think he's calming down now."

Eddie Joe's legs and arms were just twitching now and not thrashing around.

"Has this happened before?" Mrs. Gerlach asked Miss Amanda.

"Not to my knowledge, but he came by my office yesterday and told me that his head hurt. He said he'd been hit in the back of the head with a rock."

"I hope not at school."

"He didn't say where, but I think it might've happened when he was at home." She was whispering now.

About that time Eddie Joe opened his eyes and realized that he was lying on the floor.

"How'd I get down here?" He looked at Mrs. Gerlach and then at Miss Amanda.

"You weren't feeling well. Do you think you can stand up?" Mrs. Gerlach asked him.

"I think so," he said as he looked around at the rest of us with our heads on our desks.

Mr. Stinson and Miss Amanda led Eddie Joe through the classroom door.

After they left, it seemed that every hand in the class flew into the air.

Without calling on anyone, Mrs. Gerlach explained that Eddie Joe had a head injury which may have caused his seizure. She thanked all of us for praying for him. She was sure that our prayers had helped.

Eddie Joe didn't come back to school. When I asked Mrs. Gerlach how he was doing, she told me that he had moved in with another family and was going to a different elementary school.

"It's sad that he had to leave his family," I said to her.

"It's really the best thing for Eddie Joe. He'll be better off now."

"Does his new family have a bathtub?" I asked.

She looked at me and smiled a sad smile. "I feel sure they do, Bobbi. Thank you for being concerned about Eddie Joe. You were kind to him, and he needs more kindness in his life."

I never saw Eddie Joe again.

MARCH

The month of March was cool and windy. Katie, Law and I played kickball after school most days, and once a week we walked to the public library to check out some books. It still got dark pretty early, so sometimes Katie and I had to walk fast to make it to the library, choose our books and then get back home before dark.

"Mama, can Katie and I walk to town? I need some new library books. I've finished all of the ones I checked out last week."

"If you put on your coat and get home before dark," she answered.

"I will," I promised.

"Kee-Wo-Kee, K-A-T," I called to her from the bottom of her steps. She opened her door and came down the steps two at a time. She was wearing her car coat.

"Can you go?" I asked her. She nodded yes. "What about Law?"

"His grandmother said no. She thinks it's too windy today for his asthma."

"We better run to keep warm."

As we took off running down Rusk Street toward town, we passed Mr. Tressell in his truck heading toward the corner. I waved, and he gave a half-wave back.

When we reached the corner of Rusk and Adkins, we stopped to catch our breath.

"The air's real cold. It's makin' my throat hurt," Katie said.

"Breathe through your nose."

"I can't. You're runnin' too fast. I can't keep up."

"Let's walk fast then."

When we reached the library, we saw a group of grownups standing by the door talking to one another. One was pointing toward the courthouse. We leaned around the corner of the building.

"A sit-in. That's what it is. I've been readin' about those things in the newspaper," one man was telling the group.

"Why are they blockin' the door to the courthouse? Don't they know that people have business to attend to?" Miss Vera the librarian asked.

"A disgrace. That's what it is. I've never heard of such a thing. And right there in the middle of town at our beautiful old courthouse."

"I heard that the colored kids don't like it that they can't order at the Woolworth's counter or over at Fry-Hodge or at the bus station cafe."

"What makes them think they can eat at our counters?"

"They say it's their right. I don't know who put those crazy-talkin' ideas in their heads. Must be those liberal college teachers. These sit-ins have been taking place in other towns—Greensboro, Raleigh, Richmond and even in Nashville, Tennessee. That's what I heard."

"Why'd they want to go and pick Marshall."

"What other town has two colored colleges?"

"You think those are college kids over there?"

"Sure looks like it to me."

I turned to Katie and said, "I hope it's not any of Miss Lucille's students. Let's go see."

We circled around behind the library and crossed the street. At the corner near Woolworth's and North Washington, we could see colored boys and girls sitting with their arms locked together right inside of the courthouse door. It was like they were keeping watch over the Confederate soldier on the courthouse lawn.

I couldn't see all of the college students, but the ones I could see didn't look like any of the boys or girls I had seen at Miss Lucille's house. I was about to tell Katie that maybe we should leave when some white men and boys starting yelling things at the colored students. One of the boys making the most noise was the boy with bug eyes who worked at Abraham's. Another group of colored students were gathering on the courthouse lawn. The white men were yelling bad words at the students.

The colored kids weren't yelling back. They just stayed still and didn't say a word.

The next thing we knew, there were policemen and firemen with water hoses walking toward the courthouse.

"Come on," I grabbed Katie by the hand. "I'm scared."

A lot of people were yelling. Other people, even grownups were hurrying to get in their cars. We started running down North Washington. As we turned onto Rusk Street, I saw Blubber Lips ahead of us. He was walking fast. He turned to look when he heard us coming up behind him.

"Did you see all that commotion goin' on at the courthouse?" he asked.

I nodded. We had never heard his voice before. It was high like the lady singers in our church choir.

"All those people yellin' such terrible things. They should be ashamed. Those students weren't hurtin' anybody. Just makin' a statement is all."

"You think the police'll hurt 'em?" I asked him.

"I hope not. I just didn't want to stay around there waitin' to see. I'm sure it'll be all over the *News Messenger* tomorrow afternoon. You want me to walk you home? I'm goin' right by your houses."

"How do you know where we live?" Katie asked him.

"I see you most every day in the summertime."

"You never act like it. You never wave or anythin'." I said.

"I always hear you two whisperin' with that boy who has the pet squirrel. I figured you didn't like me much."

"We don't even know you, but now we do. We'll say hi from now on," I told him.

"Okay. Let's get home before dark then. I hope nothin's goin' on at Bishop."

I hadn't even thought about something bad happening at Bishop College. What about Mama and Betsy? What about Miss Lucille? I wanted to run again, but Katie was too tired.

"What's your name?" I asked him.

"Harry Price. What's yours?"

"I'm Bobbi Rogers. She's Katie Baxter. I was eleven on my birthday in February, and she just turned nine last week. How old are you?"

"I work down at the Hub Shoe Store. I'm twenty-five," he said as we walked three across on the sidewalk.

"That's pretty old," said Katie.

"Not really. I'm the youngest person at the Hub, and I sell a lot of shoes." He was bragging to us.

"We sometimes called you names when you walked by us in the summer. We shouldn't have," I said.

"Don't worry about it. I get called names a lot."

"We won't call you names anymore. Can we call you Harry, or Mr. Harry?"

"Harry. Mr. Harry sounds like my dad."

"Where's your house?" Katie asked him as she shivered from the cold wind.

"Down the street on past Bishop College."

"In colored town?" I asked him.

"Yep. In colored town. It's hard to keep my shoes shined all the time livin' on a dirt road, but as soon as I get on the sidewalk, I clean 'em off. Can't go into the Hub with dirty shoes. I'd lose my job, for sure."

"You're not colored. Why do you live in colored town?" Katie asked.

"We don't have money for a big house like yours," he said to Katie.

"I don't live in the big part—just in the upstairs part. Nona and Tada live in the big part. Our part is little, and Bobbi's house is not very big either. She sleeps in a room that used to be their garage."

"You both have pretty houses. I love those pink shutters on your house whether you live in what used to be a garage or not."

"Thanks. I bet your house is pretty, too."

"It's not, but I plan to buy my own house someday over in Dallas," he said. "I want to live in a big city—not this podunk town where colored kids can't even get a grilled cheese sandwich at Woolworth's."

"Miss Lucille moved here from Dallas. You know her? She's just a year older than you. She lives in the house on the corner."

"Don't know her. I see her sometimes outside. She's a pretty lady, but her boyfriend is an old man."

"She doesn't have a boyfriend."

"A tall fella in overalls. Sure looks like a boyfriend to me. I saw them kissin' and huggin' right outside in her side yard."

Katie looked at me and giggled. I frowned.

"When did you see that?"

"Just last week on a Saturday mornin'. I was comin' back from pickin' up some milk for my mama at the store when I heard talkin' and then saw them smoochin'."

"She see you?"

"No way. She was too in love to notice me."

Katie giggled again.

We reached her house first, so Katie said good-bye and went up the stairs to her apartment.

"Thanks for walkin' home with us," I told him. "It might be better if you not talk about Miss Lucille and her boyfriend."

"And why's that?"

"She might be embarrassed. She turns red a lot when she gets embarrassed. I take piano lessons from her, so I know."

"You know about her boyfriend then?"

"Mmm, kinda."

"I don't think you knew until I told you."

"I better go in. Mama'll be worried," I said and ran towards my house.

"See you later then," he called after me.

⊷⊷ ⊶⊶

The headlines of the *Marshall News Messenger* read "Standoff On Rights Seen." The article told all about the sit-ins that had been going on in other cities and in downtown Marshall. In all, fifty-seven colored college students had been arrested at Woolworth's or on the courthouse square on "county court charges of unlawful assembly to deprive a man of the right to do business."

The article also said that more rallies and even a parade were planned, and people were warned to stay away from the courthouse and let the authorities handle the protesters. Governor Daniel had been contacted, and some Texas Rangers were coming to Marshall to close three of the four entrances to the courthouse as a precaution. Nobody wanted the situation to get out of hand. Other articles talked about colored people wanting to end segregation in the public schools.

"Why do colored people want their kids to go to white schools?" I asked Mama after I read all of the articles in the newspaper.

"They think that white children may be gettin' a better education than colored children," she said.

"Are they?"

"I don't know that for a fact, but it could be true."

"Do you think it's wrong for colored kids to order grilled cheese sandwiches at Woolworth's?"

"I don't see what that would hurt, Bobbi, but a lot of white folks are scared of what else might happen if we allow it."

"Miss Lucille knows a lot of colored kids, and they don't seem any different to me from white kids. They like sandwiches, too."

"I'm sure they do. Things'll work themselves out. I just don't want you and Katie goin' to town on your own anymore until all of this passes over. It scared me and your daddy when you told us about all of the yellin' and the fire hoses and such. You understand me?"

"Yes, ma'am," I nodded. "Harry Price said that Miss Lucille has a boyfriend."

"Was he talkin' about Brother Billy? I see them together at church now and then."

"No. She's just friends with him. This must be somebody else."

"Well, I don't know anything about it. Why don't you ask her? You don't seem to have a problem askin' her everything else." She was teasing me.

I smiled, but I knew that I couldn't ask her about Mr. Tressell again.

APRIL

Easter Sunday was always a special day. This year the Easter Bunny brought blue and pink baby chicks to Betsy and me. Daddy said baby chicks were better than bunnies because the bunnies we got last year made a big mess, and we had to give them away. He said that the baby chicks could go live in Tada's chicken coop behind Katie's house when they outgrew their little pen in our backyard.

I helped Betsy hunt for eggs in the backyard. Our baskets were running over with eggs when Mama said it was time to eat breakfast and get ready for church.

Mama and I wore matching hats to church. Betsy had one, too, but she wouldn't keep it on her head. Daddy took a picture of his girls with the brownie camera. Then we all went to Sunday School.

During the church service, Miss Lucille played "Because He Lives" on the piano as the special music. There were a lot of "Amens" when she finished.

Brother Rutledge preached his Easter sermon about Jesus dying on the cross and then rising from the grave the third day. It was on Easter Sunday a year ago that I had walked the aisle to accept Jesus as my Savior. I had been so happy about going to heaven someday to live with Jesus that I had gone door to door to tell all of my neighbors. Brother Rutledge had even let me be baptized without a swimming cap because I told Mama I didn't mind if my hair got wet. I had too much hair to stuff inside a swimming cap, and the rubber caps smelled bad, too.

We sang all five verses of "The Old Rugged Cross," but nobody went to the front to accept Jesus or make a rededication. Brother Rutledge ended the service with the benediction and said "Happy Easter" to everyone.

After lunch, Katie, Law and I met behind Miss Lucille's garage. The strong wind had knocked down one whole side of our fort, so we had a lot of work to do to fix it. We were moving sticks and leaves out of the way when we heard a truck pull into her driveway.

It was Mr. Tressell. He didn't see us, so I didn't wave.

He got out of the truck and walked to Miss Lucille's back door. He was wearing overalls and a plaid shirt which I guessed must have been his Easter clothes. He didn't even knock. He just opened the door and went inside her house.

His truck was still there when Mama called me to come home for supper.

School started up again after the Easter holidays, and I had my regular piano lesson on Monday after school at Miss Lucille's house.

"Goin' to piano, Mama," I called out as I closed the screen door.

I noticed Miss Lucille's car was parked in her driveway and not in her garage. One of the back car doors was still open, so I closed it for her before I headed over to her house. I knocked on the back door to let her know I was there. I didn't hear her call out, so I opened the screen door.

As I stepped inside, I saw her lying with her face down on the kitchen floor. I ran over to her to see if she had fallen down. I touched her shoulder closest to me and tried to lift her arm. When I did, I screamed. There was blood all over the front of her blue blouse. Broken glass and yellow roses were all over the floor. I shook her shoulder, but she wouldn't wake up.

I ran out the door and down her back steps.

"Mama!" I screamed. "Help me, Mama! Mama!"

Mama came running out of our back door onto the patio.

"What happened? What's wrong?"

My whole body was shaking.

"Is that blood? Oh, Bobbi. Quick, lemme see your hands." She took my hands in hers and turned them over.

"It's not me. It's Miss Lucille. She's lying on the kitchen floor. There's blood all over her clothes and yellow roses and broken glass. You've gotta help her. She won't wake up. She's hurt real bad."

"Watch Betsy." She ran across the vacant lot to Miss Lucille's back door.

I watched Mama open Miss Lucille's door, and then I started crying.

It wasn't long before I heard sirens. I ran to our front window. There was a police car and an ambulance pulling up in front of Miss Lucille's house. Two policemen got out of the car, and two other men unloaded a stretcher from the ambulance. They carried it to the back door and went inside.

After a few more minutes, Detective Binotti drove up and got out of his car. He went around to the back of Miss Lucille's house, too.

Law and his grandmother came outside in their front yard under the magnolia trees to watch.

I started to cry again. I wanted Mama to come home. Betsy started to cry, too, so I went to get her out of her baby bed.

Mama came in the back door.

"Will she be all right?"

Mama put her arms around me and hugged me tight.

"Oh, Bobbi. I don't think so. She lost so much blood." Mama's face looked so sad.

"Can the doctor help her?"

She shook her head no.

"Why not? They have to help her," I couldn't stop crying. Betsy started crying again.

"She was on the floor for a while. She wasn't breathin'. I can't imagine who would do such a thing."

"Did she fall down?" I asked.

"She didn't fall. Somebody hurt her."

"Did they push her? Did she hit her head?"

"No, honey. Somebody hurt her with a knife. That's why you saw all the blood everywhere."

"Who'd do it? She was nice to everybody."

Mama put her arm around my shoulder. "I know she was. She was friendly and kind and was very sweet to you."

"She was one of my best friends even though she was a lady."

I put my head on her shoulder and started to cry again. Betsy crawled up in Mama's lap, and Daddy found us all crying when he came in the back door.

"I heard about it at the field house," he said. "I got here as soon as I could."

Mama got up and hugged Daddy.

"It's terrible, Jack. Somebody stabbed her over and over. I'm scared for all of us," she whispered to him. "The police are there and Detective Binotti, too."

"I'm goin' over there." He walked out the back door.

⚒ ⚒

Mama made chicken noodle soup for supper. She thought that might make all of us feel better. Daddy found out that whoever hurt

89

Miss Lucille must have surprised her. She had been to buy groceries. Two paper sacks of groceries were on the kitchen table and another bag with spaghetti and some canned goods was still in the car.

"Her car door was open when I went to her house, Daddy," I told him. "I closed it."

"I'll need to tell Al, Detective Binotti. You see anythin' else that was out of the ordinary?"

"No, sir. Just that. Her back door was hardly ever locked. I knocked and called her name before I went in, but she didn't answer," I said and started to cry again.

"That's enough for now, Jack. This has been a terrible day for all of us and especially Bobbi. Let's get your baths, girls, and then get to bed early."

"I'm scared. What if the bad man comes to our house?"

"You don't need to worry about that. Your daddy won't let anybody hurt you or Betsy."

"What about you, Mama?"

"Or me. Isn't that right, Jack?"

"We'll lock up tight tonight. Nobody's gonna hurt my girls. They'll have to get through me first."

"I wish I had gone over there sooner. I could've helped her," I told them.

"I know you do, but you couldn't have done anything."

"I could've yelled."

"And you might've been hurt, too." She hugged me tight.

Betsy went right to sleep after we put on our pajamas. Mama lay down beside me. I said my prayers and asked God to take good care of Miss Lucille in heaven. Then I cried myself to sleep.

Mama let me stay home from school on Tuesday. She didn't want the other kids asking me questions about Miss Lucille in case they had heard about what had happened. The policemen and Detective Binotti were at her house early and had put yellow tape around her car and across the back door and front door of her house. They didn't want anybody going inside that didn't have permission from the police.

Mama walked over and offered them some lemonade about 10:30. When she came back home, Detective Binotti was with her. He came inside.

"Bobbi, I think you met Detective Binotti when he was here about the Peepin' Tom."

"Yes ma'am," I nodded.

"Your mama tells me you found Mrs. Harris yesterday in her kitchen and that you closed her car door," he was talking soft-like to me.

"I went to my piano lesson. I go every Monday unless it's a holiday. Her car was in her driveway. It's always in her garage. The back door on her side…"

"The driver's side?" he asked.

"Yessir. That door was open. I closed it thinkin' she must've forgotten about it."

"Did you look inside the car?"

"No sir. I just closed it and went to her back door. She didn't lock her door."

"Nobody locks their doors in the neighborhood," Mama told him.

He nodded and then looked back at me. "So you went inside?"

"I knocked first and called out her name. That's what I always did. She would say, 'Come on in,' but she didn't say anything this time. I thought maybe she was talkin' on the telephone. She did that sometimes, and I would just start playin' my scales."

"So you went in the kitchen and…"

"I saw her lyin' on the floor. I was afraid she'd hit her head. I saw the glass and the yellow roses. She got some for her birthday, too."

"Roses?"

I nodded.

"And who sent the roses on her birthday?"

"A secret admirer. That's what the card said. I was there for piano when they came."

"Did she tell you who the secret admirer was?"

"She didn't know, but she was real happy."

He took a small notepad out of his shirt pocket and wrote down some notes.

"After you saw her on the floor, did you run straight home…to tell your mother?"

"I touched Miss Lucille on the shoulder first and tried to lift her arm to wake her up. That's when I saw blood all over her blouse. Some of it got on my hands. That's when I ran to tell Mama she was hurt."

"Your mama tells me you spent a lot of time with Mrs. Harris… Miss Lucille."

"I was her first piano student, and she let me practice at her house since we don't have a piano. Daddy says they're expensive."

He nodded.

"We built a fort behind her house. That's how I know she always parked her car in her garage. She didn't leave it outside. Sometimes when Mr. Tressell came, he parked in her driveway."

"Who's Mr. Tressell?"

My face got hot.

"He helped her with her garden. She wanted to grow a garden like his but smaller. He lives down the street."

"The white house with the blue door and the ramp in front," Mama explained. "His wife's in a wheelchair.

"I remember now. When I was going from house to house after the incident at the Van Worths' house, you told me they weren't mornin' people," he said to me.

"Mr. Tressell works at the railroad and goes to work at night."

"The night shift from 11- 7?"

"That's right," Mama answered.

"He came to Miss Lucille's in the summer to show her how to garden. We'd be at the fort after breakfast when he'd come. He always wears overalls. They would go in her house to get some tea when she got too hot."

"Did he come a lot to help her?"

"Yessir. She smiled a lot when he was helpin' her. He even came to see her on Easter."

"This past Sunday? Did you see him then?"

"We were at the fort playin' when he drove up."

"Did anyone else come to Miss Lucille's house to visit like Mr. Tressell did?"

"She had piano students who came after school, and some of the colored boys and girls came to practice for programs at the college."

"She teaches music at Bishop," Mama told him.

"And these colored boys came inside the house?"

"Sometimes. They liked to play the piano and sing songs. The colored boys who came trick or treatin' didn't come in the house. They just came to the door."

"How many boys came trick or treatin'?"

"Three when we were there. They were from the college. Miss Lucille knew them. I heard one say she was lookin' mighty fine."

"Were you outside then?"

"We were inside havin' popcorn balls and lemonade when they came."

"Who was with you that night?"

"Katie and Law. They live across the street. You met them before. Could it have been the Peepin' Tom?" I asked him.

"We don't know who yet, but I'm gonna find out. I think that's enough questions for today. Will it be okay if I come back to talk to you again?"

"Yessir. She was one of my best friends. I miss her, and it's only been one day."

"You've been a big help."

Mama walked him to the door. I stayed on the couch, but I could hear them talking.

"Why would somebody kill such a sweet lady?" she asked him.

"So many stab wounds. Just an awful, awful thing. Her brother took it hard. He's on his way here from Houston. I told him not to rush since we'd have to keep the body for a while. You may see him over at her house later this week."

"We'll keep an eye out. We'll want to tell him how sorry we are."

He left our house and walked to his car.

"You think I should tell Detective Binotti about Miss Lucille kissin' Mr. Tressell?" I asked Mama.

"You may need to tell him, but let's wait until his next visit. I'd sure hate to upset Mrs. Tressell if we don't have to. Just hearin' about Lucille will upset everyone on the street anyway."

Mama was right. The Van Worths and Lottie, Mavis Baxter, Sandra Sewell and Mrs. Lawrence all came over to our house that afternoon—not in a group—but one at a time. Mama told them what she knew and that I had been the one to find Miss Lucille. I mainly stayed in my room because it made me so sad to think about her lying on her floor with nobody to help her.

Our paper boy threw our newspaper on Tuesday afternoon later than he usually did. I ran out to get it. Mama said that she had better read it first. She sat down at our kitchen table while I looked over her shoulder. In big letters on the front page were the words, "Bishop College Teacher Murdered." There was a picture of Miss Lucille's house with the police tape across the doors, and underneath the picture, it said, "The stabbing took place in this house on Rusk Street."

Mama read the article and then said to me, "I'm not sure you should read this. It'll make you sad. I don't want you havin' bad dreams, Bobbi."

"I won't. I promise. Please let me read it. I have to know who hurt her," I pleaded.

"You can read it, but if it upsets you, we'll stop lookin' at the paper when it comes." Mama handed me the newspaper.

Bishop College Teacher Murdered
"Rusk Street was the scene of a heinous crime yesterday. A twenty-six year old woman who had only lived in Marshall since last June was murdered in her kitchen. She was found about 4:00 p.m. Monday afternoon lying face down on her kitchen floor with stab wounds to her back, chest, neck and face. The name of the victim was Lucille Harris. She was a widow and was a music teacher at Bishop College. She was white. Detective Al Binotti of the Marshall Police Department told this reporter that the police had some suspects they would be talking to about the murder. He asked all Marshall citizens to lock their doors and report any suspicious activity in their neighborhoods to the police department. When asked about the yellow roses at the murder scene, the detective had no comment. An unnamed source said that the colored students who had been arrested on the courthouse lawn would all be questioned by the police in regard to the murder on Rusk Street."

The article made me think of several questions I wanted to ask Mama, but she was busy cooking supper, so I took the newspaper to my room to read the article again. I knew that Miss Lucille's blouse had blood on it, but I hadn't seen the blood on her face. I had run away too fast. Who would want to stab her? None of it made sense to me.

That night at supper when Daddy said the blessing, he thanked God for Miss Lucille and the good friend she had been to our family. He prayed for her brother and his wife during these difficult days for them. He also prayed that the person who did this to her would be caught and punished very soon.

"I let Bobbi read the article in the newspaper about it today," Mama told Daddy. "I hope that was okay with you."

Daddy nodded that it was. "Bobbi girl, you know that sometimes bad things happen in the world. We don't know why, but we have to keep trusting the good Lord that he knows and that He will look after all of us."

"Why would He let someone kill Miss Lucille?" I asked.

"God gives us free will in our lives. He doesn't control all of our actions. Some people choose to follow Him and try to live good lives that are pleasin' to Him. Others choose to do wrong and please only themselves. That doesn't help us feel any better about losin' a kind lady like Miss Lucille, but we know she's in heaven now playin' the piano and leadin' the singin'. She wouldn't want you to be so sad. She'd want you to remember all of the good times you had with her, and you did have good times down at the church and at her house takin' lessons from her."

"How will I take piano lessons now, Daddy? We don't have a piano, and I don't have a teacher."

"Your mama and I will have to think about that and make some decisions directly."

"The newspaper said that the bad person cut her face. Why'd he do that?"

"That seems mighty cruel to me. He must have been really mad or crazy to do something like that to such a pretty lady, but it's hard to figure how anyone could stab someone else."

"I remember when one of your players stabbed his daddy in the leg. They sent him off to reform school, and he missed the rest of the season," I said.

"That's right. He did. Ronnie Johnson and his daddy got in a fight. His daddy had been drinkin' whisky. He was tryin' to hit Ronnie's mama, so Ronnie picked up a steak knife off of the kitchen table and stabbed him in the leg."

"Why was it bad? Ronnie was tryin' to protect his mama."

"It's against the law to stab someone, Bobbi. It's called assault."

"But he was doin' it to keep his mama from bein' hurt."

"Two wrongs don't make a right," he told me. "It would've been better for all of 'em for Ronnie to call the police instead of stabbin' his daddy."

"Who's protectin' his mama now that he's in reform school?"

"I don't know. I hope his daddy learned his lesson, but I'm not sure he did. Drinkin' whisky can lead men to do things they shouldn't do."

"Do you think the man who hurt Miss Lucille was drinkin' whisky?"

"I think that's enough talk about whisky and such," Mama said.

"Just answerin' the girl's questions. She's gotta learn sometime that there are bad people in the world, Nita."

"I think she knows that now."

I went back to school on Wednesday. Katie, Law and I were taking the short cut through colored town that morning when we saw Harry Price come out of the front door of a small wooden house. The white paint was peeling off the sides.

"Hey, Harry," I called out as I waved to him. Law acted surprised because he hadn't been with us when Harry walked us home from the courthouse sit-in. He only knew Harry as Blubber Lips.

"Hey back to you," Harry said as he walked over to us. "I heard about your neighbor gettin' killed—the pretty lady with the red hair. Who found her?"

"Bobbi did," Katie told him.

"Oh, my goodness. I had no idea it was you. That must've been worse than awful. I read all about it in the paper. Was there blood everywhere?"

I nodded my head yes. Law was staring at him.

"Why are you askin' her about it? It was horrible," Law said.

"I'm sorry. I was just so surprised it was you. Who you think did it? Her boyfriend?"

"They don't know who did it, and she didn't have a boyfriend," Katie said.

"I think maybe she did and that they should be checkin' his alibi. Gotta go. See ya later," he said as he walked toward Rusk Street.

"How'd you know his name? I don't like him," Law said.

"He's not so bad. He walked us home from town the day the colored kids had the sit-in at the courthouse. He was nice that day, wasn't he, Katie?"

"He was."

"He wasn't nice today. He shouldn't be askin' you so many questions, and why was he talkin' about a boyfriend? She didn't have a boyfriend that I know of," Law said.

We were almost to the school playground, so I took off running for the swings without answering his question. Katie and Law followed behind me.

A few of the kids in my class asked me about the murder, but most didn't seem to know that I was the one who had found Miss Lucille. The teachers at the school were all very nice to me. Some patted me on the hand, and Mrs. Gerlach even put her arm around me and gave me a hug. When I got home that afternoon, I ran out to get the newspaper. There was another article about

Miss Lucille's murder and another one about the sit-in at the courthouse. They mainly said the same thing as the other articles. "The investigation was continuing" and "the interviews with the students who had been arrested were progressing."

That same afternoon Detective Binotti came to our front door again. Mama let him in. I was doing my homework at the kitchen table.

" Detective Binotti has a few more questions for you," she told me.

"Detective, why don't you have a seat here at the table, and I'll get you a cup of coffee."

"If it's not too much bother."

"Not at all. We wanna help anyway we can."

I looked at Detective Binotti, and he smiled at me.

"I have a grandson about your age, Bobbi. He lives out in West Texas, so I don't get to see him very much. Mainly at Christmas time and in the summer when I have a week off for vacation. I wouldn't want Corky to have to go through something like this, and I'm sure sorry that you're havin' to deal with this terrible thing, but I need to see if you can help us out with this investigation."

"I'll try my best," I said softly.

"I know you will. She was your friend, and it's hard to lose a friend."

"She didn't do anything mean to anybody. Some people didn't like it that she taught at a colored school, but she told me that all kids were the same to her. She was friendly to everybody."

He took his notepad and pen out of his pocket.

"You told me that some colored boys came to her house on Halloween and made some remarks about how pretty she was."

"Three colored boys came. They said they were her students. One of them asked me if I was her daughter, and they wanted to know why I was in her house. They seemed real curious about her. They asked her why she was dressed up for Halloween, and one of them told her to look out for big bad wolves. She was dressed up like Little Red Riding Hood. She said she just wanted to be part of Halloween. The shortest boy said she was lookin' mighty fine. After she gave them their popcorn balls, they sat on the curb across from her house. One hollered out to us to watch out for goblins as we left her house. They scared us a little."

"Did you see 'em go back to her house that night?"

"No, sir, but we started runnin' when he told us to watch out for goblins."

"Did she call them by name?"

"Yessir, but I don't remember because she said the names pretty fast."

"Would you recognize 'em if you saw 'em again?"

"I think so. They were standin' on her front porch under the light."

"Alright then, let's talk about the neighbor who helped her with her garden."

"Mr. Tressell's his name."

"Right. Mr. Tressell. And he lives close to the Baxters in the house with the ramp out front?"

"Mrs. Tressell's in a wheelchair. She doesn't go anywhere, but I guess they have a ramp so she can roll outside. I've only ever seen her on her back porch or watchin' TV in her house."

"How did you see her watchin' TV?'

"We swing in Katie's hammock next to Mrs. Tressell's kitchen window. We can see her through the window rollin' around her kitchen or watchin' TV in her den."

"And the Tressells have a garden?"

"It's a big garden behind their house. Mr. Tressell's real proud of it. He told Miss Lucille all about it at the July the 4th picnic in our backyard. She asked if she could see his garden. She wanted to plant a garden, too. Her yard in Dallas wasn't big enough for one. She liked his garden so much he said he would help her grow one."

"I believe you told me that he would come to her house early in the morning to help her."

"He'd come when he got off work at the railroad early in the morning before it got too hot in the summer."

"Every day?"

"Not on Sunday. I don't think he works at the railroad on Saturday night, but Mama might know that better than me."

He looked down at his notebook.

"You mentioned that Mr. Tressell and Miss Lucille would sometimes go inside her house."

"When she got too hot, they did that. She would make them some tea to drink."

"Could you see inside her house from where you were? I believe you mentioned a fort at the back of her property."

"We couldn't see inside. Sometimes we could hear talkin', but most of the time we were playin' and couldn't hear."

"You remember how long he helped her with her garden?"

"He came a lot in the summer and some in the fall. We'd see them on our way to school. Then he stopped coming to her house. She said it was because she joined the church and that Brother Rutledge's sermon I told her about made her think about some things."

"And do you know what things she was talkin' about?"

"Brother Rutledge preached a sermon about not lettin' a bird build a nest on your shoulder, and he called the bird 'temptation.' She said that made her do some thinkin'."

Detective Binotti looked up at my mother who said, "Bobbi, maybe you should tell Detective Binotti about seein' Miss Lucille kiss Mr. Tressell."

"Do I have to? It seems like I'm tellin' secrets about her or somethin'."

"I know, but it might help find out who hurt her, and I know that you wanna do that."

"Yes, ma'am. One day I saw Miss Lucille kiss Mr. Tressell when they were standin' by his truck. They seemed all happy that day, and Harry Price who lives in colored town and works at the Hub told me he saw them kissin' in her garden one day when he was walkin' to the store. I asked Miss Lucille if Mr. Tressell could be her secret admirer, and she got all embarrassed and didn't wanna talk about it."

"Tell me more about the secret admirer. I believe you said she got some yellow roses from this secret admirer."

"On her birthday. She didn't know who sent the roses, but the card said they were from a secret admirer."

"Did someone deliver the roses to her house?"

"A man in a black car with a rainbow on the car door did. I was there for my piano lesson, and Miss Lucille was talkin' on the telephone when he came to the front door."

"Rainbow Floral, most likely," he said to Mama. She nodded.

"Do you have any other ideas about who this secret admirer might be since you and Miss Lucille were such good friends?"

"I thought maybe Brother Billy at the church could be it. They went to the movies together and talked a lot at the church, but at the Christmas program she told him she just wanted to be friends—not boyfriend and girlfriend."

"Billy Harkins?" I nodded.

"Anybody else you can think of besides Mr. Tressell and Brother Billy?"

"Only one person, but I don't know who he was. She was talkin' at her back door with someone before my lesson one day. She was tellin' him that he couldn't come inside and laughin' with him like he was teasin' her. Then she came in the house and was all red in the face. She always got red when she got embarrassed."

"But you didn't see this person, and she didn't say who he was."

I shook my head. "I think it might've been a man from the college, but it was a long time ago when I first started piano."

102

"That would've been last summer," Mama explained.

"You've been mighty helpful, Bobbi," he told me. "I'll let you get back to your homework now".

Mama walked him to the door, and he thanked her for the coffee.

"Please let us know if you find out anything," she told him.

⊷⊰⊹ ⊹⊱⊶

The newspaper on Thursday didn't have any updates on Miss Lucille's murder, but there were several articles about the sit-ins in Marshall and other towns. The headlines said, "Standoff on Rights Seen," "Pastor Held in Sit-In" and "Senate Refuses to Remove Voting Rights Section."

The Marshall reporter said in her article "that the students acting in the demonstrations were mostly from other towns. An attorney from Dallas was representing all of the students due to his experience with civil rights cases."

At supper I asked Daddy if he thought that any of the students at the sit-in could have hurt Miss Lucille.

"I don't think so, Bobbi girl. The paper said they were mostly from out of town, so I don't see how they would've known her. My guess is it was someone she knew either from the college or from somewhere else in town. She was a mighty pretty lady. I'm sure a lot of people noticed her, and with her bein' a widow lady, people would've known that she lived alone."

"You think it could've been a robber?"

He shook his head and said, "She didn't seem to have anything of any value except for that piano, and nobody could steal it very easy. She was like the rest of us—just tryin' to get by. The police'll figure it out."

"You think it could've been the Peepin' Tom? Detective Binotti didn't mention him when he came by again."

"What did he mention?" he asked Mama. "Does he have any leads?"

"He mainly wanted to ask Bobbi some more questions about the boys from Bishop and about Mr. Tressell."

"What about Jim Tressell?"

"Well, he was helpin' her with her garden and accordin' to Bobbi," she said as she smiled at me, "they spent a lot of time together both inside and outside her house."

"Do you mean to tell me that a married man was spendin' time inside her house on a regular basis?"

"He was helpin' her in the garden, and then they would go in to have something cool to drink. You know how hot it can get."

"Things might have been gettin' hot inside, too," he said. I saw Mama frown.

"We best let the police do their work. Pass your daddy some more mashed potatoes please, Bobbi."

Miss Lucille's brother and his wife arrived at her house on Friday afternoon. We saw them drive up in a tan Plymouth sedan and park in the driveway behind her house. When they got out of their car, I saw that he had red hair just like Miss Lucille. He was tall like she was, too. His wife was a lot shorter and had curly brown hair. She didn't act like she wanted to go inside the house, but he put his left arm around her shoulders. He pulled the yellow tape to the side, and they went in through the back door.

After they had been inside for half an hour or more, Mama asked if I would like to go over to meet them. I said yes, so she combed her hair and changed Betsy's diaper. She reminded me to mind my manners during our visit. We headed across the vacant lot between our house and hers to meet Miss Lucille's kinfolk. Her brother, Larry, invited us inside. I didn't really want to look at the kitchen floor where I had seen Miss Lucille the day I found her lying there, but I couldn't help myself. Someone must have cleaned up the blood and the broken glass and thrown away the roses. It didn't look like anything bad had happened in there at all.

He introduced his wife as Patty. She was very quiet. When she went to the kitchen to get some tea for Mama and lemonade for Betsy and me, Larry told us that Patty was really upset. They were both having a hard time dealing with the loss of William and now Miss Lucille. They had thought that moving to a small town would be good for her. They were planning to pack up all of Miss Lucille's things and make arrangements to take her body to Dallas to be buried next to William. Mama asked if there would be any kind of service in Marshall, and he said no. They didn't want all of the gawkers that turn out after a murder.

Mama asked Larry if they were planning to keep Miss Lucille's piano, and he said that they were going to sell it since they didn't have room for it at their place in Houston. I was surprised when Mama said that she and Daddy might like to buy it if they could work out a way to pay it out. As we left Larry told Mama that he would think about a price and get back with her.

I was happy that Baldwin might be coming to stay at our house.

The following week we were swinging in the hammock in Katie's side yard when I saw Detective Binotti pull up and park his car in front of the Tressells' house. He got out and walked to their front door. In a few minutes we saw him walk out onto the back porch and then into the garden.

Mr. Tressell mostly looked down at the ground while Detective Binotti was talking to him. Mr. Tressell nodded his head yes several times, and then the two of them headed back toward the house.

I saw Mrs. Tressell sitting in her wheelchair on the back porch watching them.

Detective Binotti left the garden through the side gate and stopped to say hello to us on the way to his truck.

"Hey there. Nice day for swingin' in a hammock if you ask me. If I was your age, that's what I'd be doin'."

"You askin' Mr. Tressell some questions?" Law asked him.

"That I am," he replied. "Hopin' he can be of assistance with our investigation."

"Did he do it? Meme said he prob'ly got jealous and killed her," Law told him.

I looked at Law with my mouth wide open. What was he talking about? Where did his grandmother get that kind of idea?

"We're askin' lots of people questions, son. Not ready to make any arrests yet."

"He didn't do it," I said to all of them. "They were good friends."

"Meme said they were more than friends. She says all kinds of terrible things were goin' on in that house—from colored kids comin' over to sinful things between a man and a woman."

"You don't even know what you're talkin' about, Law Miller. I can't believe your grandmother would be talkin' like that to you," I told him.

"Meme was talkin' on the telephone, and I heard her say it."

"She never liked Miss Lucille." I was mad at him.

"Okay, kids. No need to get in a huff here. There's always a lot of talk after a murder. Just so you know, most of it's wrong. I better be on my way," he said as he tipped his white hat at us.

"I'm goin' home," I told my friends.

"You don't have to get mad at me," Law called out as I ran across the street.

I opened the front door to our house and went straight to my room. Mama heard me come in and came to check on me. I was lying on my bed.

"Somethin' happen, Bobbi? You never come in before I call you."

"Law said some mean things about Miss Lucille to Detective Binotti when he came to see Mr. Tressell."

"When was this?"

"Just a few minutes ago. He talked to Mr. Tressell in his garden while we were swingin' in the hammock. Then he said hello to us as he was leavin', and Law told him his grandmother said that Miss Lucille was sinnin'. Why'd she say that?"

"When people are scared, and someone gets murdered right here on our street, people say and do things that they shouldn't. They want an answer, so they make one up."

"She said Mr. Tressell killed her." I started to cry.

Mama came over to the bed and rubbed my back.

"I'm sorry, honey. We never want to think bad of anyone."

"But they were friends. He helped her. Mrs. Lawrence told someone on the telephone that they were doin' sinful things between a man and a woman. They wouldn't do that, would they?"

"No one knows what other people might do in certain circumstances, but it's best for us to remember Miss Lucille as the wonderful friend she was to you and to all of us. I better get dinner goin' for your daddy. You rest a while, and then you'll feel better."

I didn't think so.

MAY

The stories in the paper about the sit-in at the courthouse did not die down over the next few weeks. In all sixty-seven students had been arrested. Ten of them were from Wiley College, and ten were from Bishop College. Three were fined $200, and thirty-two were fined $50. One hundred fifty people had been held for a short time according to the reporter.

There weren't any more articles about Miss Lucille. Some of our neighbors called Mama and asked for updates, but we didn't know anything new. Daddy and Mama bought the piano from Miss Lucille's brother on a layaway plan. Daddy asked some of his football players to help him move it to our house. It was on rollers, but getting it down Miss Lucille's two front steps and up our three front steps wasn't easy. As soon as "Baldwin" was positioned opposite the green sofa in our living room, I sat down to play. I was very sad that Miss Lucille wasn't there to hear me, but I was happy that her piano was now mine. Mama was still asking around about a good piano teacher for the fall.

Daddy and the team were having spring two-a-day practices at the football field, and he came home one night with some news from Detective Binotti. He had run into him at the post office early that morning before he went to the field house and had asked him how the investigation was going.

"Al told me that the three colored boys who Bobbi saw on Halloween all had alibis. When the police went to Bishop to look for the boys, they voluntarily came forward and said they had been to her house on Halloween night. They got popcorn balls, sat down on the curb to eat them and then went back to the college. He said they couldn't have been involved in the murder because they were on Easter break and didn't get back to the college until late on Monday afternoon. The dorms have a check-in time sheet, and friends of the boys were ridin' in the car with them. They wouldn't have gotten back into Marshall until after Bobbi went over to her house that day," Daddy said.

"Did he say if they asked any other boys at Bishop any questions—like boys from the sit-in?" Mama asked.

"He didn't mention the sit-in, but he did say that no one at Bishop had heard anyone talkin' about the murder other than to say it happened close to the school. He said that in his experience, someone usually lets something slip or brags about takin' part by now."

"Why would someone brag about a stabbin', Daddy?"

"Honey, I can't answer that. Since we can't imagine stabbin' anybody, we sure can't imagine braggin' about it."

"He said they're still tryin' to come up with a motive for the killin'. She could've been resistin' someone's advances toward her—a student or another teacher, but no one knows who that might be. Mostly, he said everyone at Bishop misses her."

"Just like we do. What about Brother Billy? Did he mention him?"

"He did. Brother Billy was at work that day at the church. They think that Lucille was killed between 8 a.m. and noon that day, so he was ruled out as a suspect."

"I never thought he could've killed her anyway," said Mama. "He's a Christian man and is on the staff at the church. I hope them questionin' him doesn't hurt his reputation with the church people."

"I don't see how it would since they don't think he did it. I never did see how he could kill her—a silly man like that," Daddy said.

"Hush, Jack. He works with the youth at the church. Bobbi will be in his youth group in a couple of years."

"I know that. He's still silly if you ask me."

"Did Detective Binotti say anything about Mr. Tressell?" I asked not really wanting to hear his answer.

"He did. Since Jim was the last one seen at her house on Easter, he has to be treated like a suspect."

"He wouldn't hurt her, Daddy. He was always so nice to her."

"They haven't found the knife yet. The killer must have taken it with him, and it looks bad for him that Jim doesn't seem to have an alibi. He said that he and his wife were at home asleep. He got home from work about 7:15 that morning, took a shower and went to sleep. His wife was asleep on their couch. She did that sometimes. Seems it's easier for her to get on the couch from her wheelchair. She can't say for sure that he was in their bed, but she thinks he was. Al said Jim doesn't have many answers for their questions—never has been much of a talker. I don't think we should be surprised if they arrest him since we know that he and Lucille were very close friends." He raised his eyebrows and looked at Mama when he said that last part about close friends.

"I hope they don't," I said. "He didn't do it."

"Bobbi girl, I hope you're right."

"We'll all hold a good thought for him," Mama added.

The red and white spring football game was a big success. Everyone was sure that we would win district and even go to state in the fall. The school year was winding down. We were practicing for our end-of-the year program which was mainly patriotic music. We would all be waving flags and singing, "God Bless America," even though most people seemed pretty worried about the Freedom Rides that were happening in the country. The first Freedom Ride had taken place in early May.

The newspaper had articles all about the Freedom Rides, and I read every one of them. James Farmer, Jr. who was from Marshall was one of the planners. There were thirteen riders. Seven of them were colored, and six of them were white. They thought that colored people should be allowed to ride on Greyhound and Trailways buses with white people and sit wherever they wanted to sit. The paper said that their plan was to have at least one colored person sit with a white person on the bus and at least one colored rider sit up front where seats were reserved for white people. There wasn't any trouble until John Lewis was attacked in South Carolina, and some riders were arrested in North Carolina and Mississippi.

Things got worse when the riders got to Birmingham, Alabama on Mother's Day. They were attacked by members of the Ku Klux Klan who tried to burn their bus, and then they beat the riders as they were trying to get out of the burning bus. Some of the riders had to go to the hospital, but some of the white hospitals wouldn't take them. Attorney General Robert Kennedy, the President's brother, sent a man to meet with the riders and with the police to keep the riders safe, but the bus drivers were afraid to drive them anymore. The riders were taken to an airplane, and after a bomb threat that made everyone get off the airplane, they got back on the airplane and were flown to New Orleans. About a week later a group of ten colored students rode a bus from Nashville to Birmingham where they were put in jail. They sang freedom songs all the time while they were in jail, so the Police Commissioner let them out of jail and drove them back to Tennessee.

Mama was combing my hair the night of the school program when I asked her what she thought about the Freedom Riders.

"You've been readin' the paper again, haven't you?"

"Yes, ma'am. Ever since Miss Lucille was hurt, I like to read it. There's never anythin' about her anymore, but there's a lot in the paper about the Freedom Riders. Why do they have to sit at the back of the bus?"

"It's sad, but a lot of people in the South don't like colored people thinkin' they're the same as white people. I don't agree with that thinkin', but I'm in the minority around these parts, so I don't talk about it much, and it'd be better if you not talk about it either."

"I know Katie's daddy hates colored people," I said.

"I don't know if it's right to say he hates all colored people, but he doesn't want them gettin' out of their place."

"Why do people think they're different from us."

"Just the color of their skin, is all," she said. "The Bible tells us to love everyone no matter what color of skin they have or what they look like or how they treat us. It's not easy to do, but if we want to be like Jesus, that's what we should do."

"Jesus loves all colors of children. We sing about it at Sunday School."

"I know you do. I've learned that some people don't ever want anything to change, Bobbi. I don't want you to be one of those people. Like I've always told you—live by the Golden Rule—and everything will turn out all right. Treat other people—all other people—like you wanna be treated, and they'll treat you right. I don't know anymore than you do about the Freedom Riders, but I know it's not right for people to beat 'em or scream at 'em or try to set their bus on fire just because they wanna sit wherever they want to on a bus."

That night at the school program, there were a lot of grownups saying that the Freedom Rides would most likely continue and that things were bound to get worse during the summer.

Things got worse for Mr. Tressell, too.

JUNE

Katie, Law and I were playing hide 'n seek in her backyard on Saturday morning when I decided to hide in the chicken house. The chicken house was about half the size of our whole house. Tada had built two long rows of shelves in the back part for the chickens to nest and lay their eggs. The wood floors back there were usually covered with chicken poop. The whole house had screens on the windows. In the front part of the chicken house near the door was where Tada kept his tools, feed sacks and buckets that he used for feeding the chickens. All of the chickens were outside in the yard this morning, so I didn't think that Katie and Law would think of looking for me inside the chicken house.

I had been hiding for almost ten minutes waiting for them to find me when I got bored and started looking under some feed sacks that were stacked beside the screen door. When I looked under the second feed sack, I saw a dirty rag underneath it. I leaned over to get a better look and realized that the rag was wrapped around something long and hard. Without thinking much about it, I picked up the rag and opened the door to the chicken house.

Katie and Law said were sitting on her back porch steps waiting for me to give myself up. When they saw me, they came running over to see what I was holding in my hands.

"Where were you?" Law asked. "We got tired of lookin' for you. You always hide too hard. What's that?"

"I was hidin' in there in the chicken house, and I found it."

"Inside with all the chicken poop? I bet you smell bad now."

"I do not."

"What's in it?" Katie asked about the dirty rag.

"It's heavy is all I know. Let's unwrap it."

"Should we ask Tada first?" Law asked.

"He's at work. It's prob'ly just an old hammer or somethin' he uses to fix things in the chicken house, but it's kinda like a Nancy Drew mystery." I slowly lifted part of the dirty rag.

"It's a knife!" Katie yelled.

"It looks dirty, too," said Law.

"Or maybe that's blood on it from when Tada kills chickens," I said.

"Or it could be the knife that killed Miss Lucille," Law said.

I dropped it on the ground—rag and all.

"Why'd you do that?" he asked.

"I don't wanna touch the knife that hurt her."

"You better pick it up. We better show your mama."

"You pick it up."

Law wrapped the dirty rag back around the knife, and Katie and I followed behind him as the three of us walked slowly to my house. Mama was in the den ironing clothes when we came in through the back patio door.

"What're you three up to?" she asked. Then she saw that Law was holding something out towards her. "What's that, Law?"

"Bobbi found it in the chicken house. We were playin' hide and seek, and she found it. It's a knife with a lot of dirt or somethin' on it."

"Let me see it," she said as she set her iron down on the ironing board. "Put it on the table there." She pointed at the kitchen table.

In the kitchen light, you could tell the rag was a kitchen towel that you would use for drying dishes. The edges were ragged, and the yellow and white stripes were faded. Mama opened the rag carefully and caught her breath when she saw the knife.

"It's a knife."

"Why would it be in the chicken house?" I asked her. "Would Tada use it there?"

"I don't think so. We'll have to ask him though to be sure. Where'd you say you found it?"

"It was under a feed sack on top of an old wood box. I was lookin' around in the chicken house while I was waitin' for them to find me," I said as I looked at Katie and Law. "I was hidin' in there."

"Let's leave it here for now. It's best if we not touch it, I think, and we'll ask Tada about it as soon as he gets home," she told us. "Go on back outside now."

We went to the fort to play. There was a "For Lease" sign in front of Miss Lucille's house, and her house was closed up tight. All the window shades in the bedroom were pulled all the way down.

We forgot about the knife as we went about our business defending our fort until Mama called me to come to lunch.

"See ya after lunch," I called to Katie and Law.

When I came into the kitchen, Mama was talking on the telephone.

I heard her say, "It's right here on our kitchen table. I'll be home all afternoon. Anytime you wanna come is fine."

"Who was that you were talkin' to?" I asked as I sat down at the table.

Mama put plates of hot dogs and potato chips in front of Betsy and me. Betsy's wiener was cut into small pieces. Mine had a bun and a lot of mayonnaise just like I liked it.

"That was Detective Binotti. He's gonna come by to take a look at what you found this mornin' in the chicken house."

"Did you ask Tada?"

"Not yet, but I called Mavis, and she said that Tada and Nona don't own any Cutco knives, so that made me think of callin' the detective."

"What's a Cutco?"

"A special kind of knife that men sell door-to-door. The name is always engraved on the blade."

"Could it be the knife that…" I couldn't finish my question.

"It's possible, but it's best to let the police take a look at it before we go thinkin' that for sure," she told me.

"Why would it be in Tada's chicken house?"

"It doesn't make any sense to me unless someone was hidin' it there."

"But I found it."

"I know you did, but it has been a while since…Easter."

"Like it was a good hidin' place."

"Like that, yes," she nodded as she sat down to eat a hot dog with us.

We were clearing the dishes off the table when someone knocked on the door. I ran to see who it was. Detective Binotti was standing on our small front porch looking across the street at the Baxters' house.

I opened the screen door, and he turned around to face me.

"Hi there, Bobbi. Is your mother home?"

"She's in the kitchen. We just finished eatin' hot dogs."

"Sounds like a good lunch to me," he said and followed me inside.

"You got here mighty fast, Detective," Mama said.

"Not much traffic between here and the jail house. That it?" he asked and nodded his head toward the yellow and white dish towel on our wooden kitchen table.

"That's it. Like I said on the telephone, Bobbi found it in the Baxters' chicken house. You know how kids play hide 'n seek? They were doin' that this mornin'."

"It was under a feed sack. I was just lookin' around. Katie and Law were havin' trouble findin' me. It was a good hidin' place."

"It was a good hidin' place," he agreed as he picked up the dish towel. I noticed he was wearing plastic gloves. He opened the top part of the dish towel that was folded over and looked closely at the knife.

"It's a Cutco," Mama said. "We don't have any. A door-to-door salesman came to the house last fall tryin' to sell me one, but they're expensive. The name's right there on the blade."

"Uh huh," he said as he lifted the knife carefully out of the dishcloth. He was holding it up to the light. "I'm gonna take this to the station, and then I'll be back to let Bobbi show me exactly where she found it."

"Could it be what you've been lookin' for?" Mama asked the detective as he was wrapping the dishcloth around the knife again. He slid it inside a plastic bag.

"Looks like it to me. We'll need to check it for fingerprints," he said. "I can see myself out. We appreciate your call, Mrs. Rogers. Say hello to Coach for me."

"Bobbi'll be around when you need her. Just let us know."

He waved and said, "Thank you, ma'am."

⊶ ⊷

Detective Binotti came back that same afternoon. He had two policemen with him. He asked me to show him where I found the dish towel and the knife.

"Did you or the other kids touch the knife or play with it?"

"No, sir. As soon as Law unwrapped the top of the towel, and we saw it was a knife, I dropped it on the ground. It was still in the rag though, so it didn't get any more dirt on it or anythin'."

The other two policemen were looking all around inside the chicken house which caused the chickens who were on their nests to make a lot of racket.

"You and your friends play in here a lot?"

"No, sir. That's why I knew it was a good hidin' place. Just Tada comes in here with the chickens every day."

"I know you keep a good eye on things here in the neighborhood. Did you ever see anybody else come in the chicken house? Mr. Tressell's house is pretty close to it."

"No, sir. Not even Katie's dad comes in here. Everybody knows these are Tada's chickens. Mr. Tressell wouldn't have any need to come in here, would he?"

"No reason that I can think of. Ever see any colored boys 'round here?"

"No, sir. The chickens would prob'ly scare 'em to death with all the noise they make."

"That would cause a ruckus," he said smiling at me. "Thanks for your help again, Bobbi. I'm guessin' you might make a good detective someday."

⊨⊰ ⊱⊨

Less than a week later right before lunch on a Thursday, we were swinging in the hammock when Detective Binotti and the same two policemen who had been with him the week before drove up and parked in front of the Tressells' house. The policemen walked a couple of steps behind him up the front steps to the door. We stopped swinging and sat down on the curb to watch what would happen next.

When Mr. Tressell opened the door, we heard Detective Binotti say, "Jim Tressell, you're under arrest for the murder of Lucille Harris. If you cannot afford an attorney, one will be provided for you. You'll need to come with us now."

We heard Mr. Tressell say, "Can I get my things?"

"You won't be needin' much. You best leave anything of any value here with your wife."

"You takin' him to jail?" Mrs. Tressell called out to the detective.

"Yes, ma'am. We are. You can visit him there."

"And how would I be doin' that?" she asked him.

"Well, that's where he'll be. Come along now, Jim." Detective Binotti led him to the car and put him in the back seat. I saw him sitting next to Mr. Tressell as the car pulled away from the curb. We heard the front door to the Tressells house slam with a loud bang.

"I better go tell Mama," I said to Katie and Law. As I stood up to leave, I saw Mrs. Tressell staring out her front window at me.

⊷⊱ ⊰⊶

Pictures of Mr. Tressell and Miss Lucille were on the front page of the newspaper under the headline that read "Neighbor Arrested for Murder of Teacher." The reporter said that the police department had in their possession the bloody knife they believed was used to commit the murder. It was found by some children playing near the home of the suspect and was wrapped in a dish towel. Fingerprints had been taken from the knife, and investigators had determined that the Tressells had purchased two Cutco knives, Double D-edge Trimmers, from a door-to-door salesman back in September. The salesman remembered them because Mrs. Tressell was in a wheelchair. He hadn't sold knives to any other families on Rusk Street. The reporter explained that a number of suspects had been questioned, and everyone but Mr. Tressell had an alibi. He then repeated all of the details from the other articles that had been printed in the newspaper before about Miss Lucille and the attack on her. Detective Binotti was quoted as saying "that neighbors should be able to rest easier now. He thanked people in the community for their help in leading to the arrest of Jim Tressell for murder."

At dinner that night Daddy told Mama that he still couldn't believe Mr. Tressell would kill anyone.

"Seems like such a regular guy. Hard to believe that he could do somethin' so terrible. Some of the guys at the field house keep sayin' that they thought for sure it was one of the colored boys from the college, but Al told me himself that those boys had alibis, so I guess the police know what's right."

"I can't believe it either. He's been comin' to our picnics for years. He never said much but seemed like a nice man. It's so sad that Ruth is alone in that wheelchair. I wonder how she's gettin' around now and what she'll do about groceries. Maybe I should go by to check on her," Mama told him.

"Why don't you wait a day or so and then go by. She may not want any visitors right now after this shock."

I wasn't very hungry and asked to be excused.

I went to my piano, but before I started playing, I heard Daddy say, "My guess is she broke up with him again, and he didn't like it. Didn't want her findin' another man. She was a good lookin' woman, for sure."

"I don't think we should talk about it in front of Bobbi. She can't believe he would kill her. She saw them as good friends. She can't even imagine that he was her boyfriend. You and I know they were havin' an affair. I'm not sure I should let her keep readin' the paper every day."

"Girl has to start growin' up sometime, Nita. I don't see any harm in lettin' her read the paper. They won't give too many details in there."

"I don't know about that. You know how reporters love to tell all the gory details."

"Well, you read it first and then decide. You know best about girls."

"I can't imagine how devastatin' this must be for Ruth. I hope she has some family to come help her."

"You'll know more when you visit. She might need someone to talk to. You may find out more than you wanna know."

"I doubt that," Mama told him.

When they stopped talking, I started playing "Sweet Hour of Prayer." I knew that both of the Tressells needed prayers now more than ever.

The only other article in the newspaper during the week said that Mr. Tressell couldn't post bond and would stay in jail. The court had appointed an attorney to represent him. District Attorney Mack Craig said that he planned to seek the death penalty in the case and that details about the murder would all be brought out during the trial. He hoped to be ready to go to trial in August.

Two days later Mama asked Mavis if she would come over to our house to watch Betsy while she went to visit Ruth Tressell. Mavis brought Annie with her, and the two little girls played inside while Katie, Law and I played kickball in our backyard.

When Mama got back home, I asked Katie and Law if they wanted to go inside for some lemonade. We were all really hot, but I also wanted to find out what Mrs. Tressell had told Mama.

Mama and Mavis were sitting at the kitchen table drinking iced tea.

"Do we have any lemonade?"

"In the ice box."

I poured three lemonades, and we sat down on the floor. I got out our Monopoly game, and we chose our pieces. I always picked the car. Katie chose the shoe, and the battleship was Law's favorite. As the banker, I divided the play money, and we rolled the dice.

Mama and Mavis talked as we played. Annie and Betsy were playing with some baby dolls and colored plastic blocks in the playpen.

"How's she doin'?" Mavis asked.

"I guess all right considerin' the circumstances. At first, when she came to the door, she didn't say much. I wasn't sure she was gonna invite me in. Maybe she thought I was just bein' nosy, but I told her I wanted to help if I could and how sorry I was about the whole situation. After that she unlatched the screen and asked me to come in. I realized that was the first time I've ever been inside their house. I felt bad that I'd never baked her a pie. They were livin' on Rusk Street before we moved here, so I guess I never really thought about it. The house is really small, but maybe that's a good thing since she can't get around very well. They have the furniture pushed back against the walls, you know, so that her wheelchair can roll from room to room."

"Has she been to see him at the jail yet?" Mavis asked.

"She didn't mention it if she has, and I didn't ask. I said what a shock it was to all of us and that we always thought of him as such a nice, quiet man when he came to our picnics on the Fourth of July. She thanked me for that."

"Did she say if any family is comin' to help her?"

"I asked about her family, but she said that she didn't have any, and his family was horrified that he's been arrested for murder. She acted like most of them didn't live close by except for one niece who lives over in Spring Hill. She's plannin' to come help her on the weekends. I told her I'd be happy to pick up some things for her when I make my weekly grocery run, and she said that would be a big help to her. We visited a little about the weather and the garden. She seemed concerned about who might look after the garden now that Jim was in jail. I tried to be encouragin' to her and told her that we hoped they had the wrong man, so he could get out soon."

"Did that make her feel better?"

"I don't think so because she started to cry then. I was sorry I'd upset her. I went to the kitchen to get her a glass of water and a tissue. Right there on the counter was another Cutco knife. She must have been slicin' vegetables when I knocked on her door. It made me think that the police might be right about the knife the kids found in the chicken house."

"The paper said they're testin' it for fingerprints. That may wrap up the case for good if his fingerprints are on it."

"She's always seemed like such a sad lady, and now this, on top of her illness, doesn't seem fair. I wish someone else's fingerprints would be on that knife. He never seemed like a killer to me, but Jack says that you never know what some people will do when they think they might lose the person they love."

"Howard doesn't have any doubt he did it. He never thought it was right for Jim Tressell to be spendin' so much time in her garden. Katie would tell us last summer that he was there an awful lot."

"What about me?" Katie asked Mavis.

"Nothin' child. You don't need to be listenin' to us talk. Anybody land on Park Place yet?"

"Not yet," Katie told her. "Law's the closest to it."

Mama and Mavis started talking again only this time a little quieter.

"Mrs. Lawrence called me one day real upset because she saw him goin' in the back door when she was comin' home from the store. You'd think that they might've tried to be more secretive," said Mavis in almost a whisper.

"Maybe they weren't secretive because they weren't doin' anything wrong. I know I sound like Pollyanna, but it does seem strange that they wouldn't hide it better." Mama's voice was very low.

"Howard says lust makes people lose their minds. Their thinkin' becomes all fuzzy."

"I still can't believe he'd stab her. Why would anyone kill someone they supposedly love?"

"Didn't you say she had stopped him from comin' over once before?"

I saw Mama nod her head. "After she joined the church. You remember when she went out with Brother Billy a few times. I hoped they'd hit it off, but Bobbi told me she just wanted to be friends with him."

"Seemed like a good match to me. If that had worked, she might still be alive."

"If only," added Mama.

"What happened after you got Ruth the water and tissue?"

"She wiped her eyes and told me she was tired. I took that as the signal I should leave. I said I'd come by next week to get her grocery list when I was goin' to Abraham's. She asked me to call her first."

"What'll she do for money? Do you think the railroad will keep payin' him while he's in jail?"

"I would hope so. Innocent until proven guilty, and he's worked there a long time. Maybe the Tressells have saved some money. They don't live high on the hog. That's for sure."

Mavis looked at the rooster clock on our kitchen wall and said, "I better be headin' home to start supper. Thanks for fillin' me in."

"Thank you for watchin' the kids."

"Katie, you come on home in a little while," said Mavis as she and Annie went out the back door.

"I will. Law's winnin' anyway. He always wins at Monopoly."

JULY

Our July the 4th picnic was not as much fun this year. Everyone was talking about Miss Lucille's murder and the upcoming trial. Daddy cooked barbecue chicken and ribs on his grill, and Mr. Sewell brought a watermelon like he always did, but the ladies acted nervous and the men talked in low voices.

Katie, Law and I played in the sand box that was next to Daddy's backyard tool shed. We weren't going to our fort anymore since it was at the back of Miss Lucille's yard. Mama didn't want us to play anywhere but in one of our own yards. We still went to swing in the hammock between Katie's house and Mr. Tressell's house. Sometimes we could see Mrs. Tressell watching television. I felt sad for her. So did the ladies at the picnic.

"I can't imagine what I would do if Howard had killed somebody," Mavis told Mama and Mrs. Lawrence. Mama was tossing a green salad, and Mavis was filling plastic cups with ice. Mrs. Lawrence was watching them work. Law's mother and stepfather hadn't arrived yet.

"I knew that floozy was trouble from the day she moved to our street," said Law's grandmother. "The way she wore those short shorts. She should've been ashamed. Just askin' for trouble, if you ask me."

Mama looked our way to see if I had heard. I kept playing with my little plastic men in the sand box. Law was building a moat, and Katie was filling it with water from a bucket. As soon as she poured the water, it drained right through the sand.

"I liked her," Mama said. "She didn't mean to cause any trouble—just a lonely lady and a young one, too. She was really nice to Bobbi."

"Maybe she was, but she should've kept her hands off that married man."

"He's the one on trial for murder, Mrs. Lawrence. Seems to me he should've kept his hands to himself. He has a wife at home," said Mavis.

"Men can't help themselves. Women have to be the ones to say no."

"That doesn't seem right to me," added Mama. "It takes two to tango."

"And now one of them is dead, and one is a murderer," said Mrs. Lawrence.

"Innocent until proven guilty," Mama told her.

"Innocent, my foot. Just wait until the trial. He's guilty, and she brought it on herself. Now that poor Ruth Tressell doesn't have a husband. He's been in jail since they came to arrest him."

"Nita checks in on her once a week and picks up some groceries for her, and his niece comes to help a couple of times a month," said Mavis.

"Nice of you to do it, Nita. I don't even like Law playin' near that floozy's house. Immoral things were goin' on in there. I just know it."

"Well, it's all closed up now."

"And I bet nobody will want to lease it either since it's a murder house," said Mrs. Lawrence.

"I haven't seen anybody lookin' at it," added Mama. "Maybe once the trial is over, somebody will be interested."

"I sincerely doubt it. You know I used to see his truck parked in her backyard. Couldn't see what they were doin' in that garden of hers, but his truck was there an awful lot. Way too often. Nita, you should've said somethin' to her. I know you let Bobbi spend time in there takin' those piano lessons. Seems to me you would've wanted a lady with morals teachin' your child."

"I wish I'd been a better friend to her. I hate to mess in other people's business, but she might still be alive if I'd talked to her about spendin' too much time with him."

"You can't blame yourself, Nita," said Mavis, "and she wasn't a bad influence on Bobbi. The girl thought highly of her."

Mrs. Lawrence just shook her head from side to side.

"To tell you the truth," said Mavis as she buttered corn on the cob, "I never heard him say more than two words, but I guess he must've talked to Lucille."

"He always reminded me of Paul Newman."

"Now that you mention it, I can see the Paul Newman resemblance," Mavis said to Mama.

"He never said much to any of us, but he did have those pretty blue eyes."

Daddy walked up then and asked, "Who had pretty blue eyes?"

"Jim Tressell."

"He still has those blue eyes, I reckon. You're talkin' like he was dead, too."

"Well, he will be when they send him to the electric chair," said Mrs. Lawrence.

"Bobbi, you, Law and Katie, go help Tada and Nona with the food they're carryin'," called out Mavis. I think she didn't want us to hear what Mrs. Lawrence was saying, but we had already heard too much. I wasn't even hungry for Daddy's barbecue chicken anymore.

AUGUST

M r. Tressell's trial started on the hottest day of the year. The temperature hit 102 degrees on August 16th. Mama and I walked up the steps of the courthouse and entered through the same door where I'd seen the college kids during the sit-in back in the spring. That seemed like a long time ago now.

Mavis was looking after Betsy since Daddy had already started fall football practice. Yesterday I overheard him tell Mama that he didn't think it was a good idea for her to take me along to the trial, but she said that I could hear the opening statements since most of what they would say had probably already been in the newspaper.

Everybody in the courtroom was fanning—trying their best to keep cool. Mama and I found a place to sit on the back row. The courtroom was not as big as I thought it would be. There were twenty wooden rows—like pews at our church but without cushions—on each side facing the place where the judge would sit. There was one wide aisle down the middle. The walls were painted white although they looked pretty dirty to me. The ceiling was tall and four fans were spinning overhead. I had watched a lot of episodes of Perry Mason on television, so I knew pretty much what to expect from a trial.

I saw Miss Lucille's brother Larry sitting in the first row behind the district attorney's table. His red hair made him stand out. His wife Patty was sitting beside him. She was fanning herself with one of those paper fans that had a pretty picture on it.

As District Judge James Harper walked into the courtroom, the bailiff said, "All rise," and we all stood up. The judge was wearing a long black robe. I was thinking that he must be even hotter than we were with that robe over his clothes. He had wavy silver hair, and when he sat down in his chair, a bright light was right over his head. It made the top of his hair shine which was kind of spooky. He looked out over all of us in the courtroom. Everyone was very quiet and serious. I was wearing my best summer Sunday dress, and Mama was dressed in a green cotton dress with a white collar. It wasn't every day that we went to a trial. We were both sitting up straight.

The twelve people on the jury came into the courtroom next. They were all men. Most of them looked older than Daddy. They were all wearing ties, short–sleeved shirts and dark trousers. I saw a couple of them pulling on their ties. They took their seats in the jury box and looked at the judge who made some announcements to all of us about how to behave in the courtroom, and then the trial got under way.

District Attorney Mack Craig stood up and walked over to face the jury. He was a tall man with dark brown hair which was combed in a way that Mama called "unruly." He was wearing a blue and green striped tie and a black suit. His white shirt was already wet around the top of his collar. His voice filled up the courtroom when he said, "Thank you, Your Honor. Gentlemen of the jury, my name is Mack Craig, and as the duly elected district attorney here, it's my responsibility to bring this case before you. Jim Tressell, one of our Marshall citizens who works down at the T

& P Railroad, is accused of the heinous murder of Lucille Harris, a twenty-six year old teacher at Bishop College. During this trial we'll tell you about the secret affair he was having with the victim, about the murder weapon he used to stab her and about his motive. She wanted to break off the affair, and he didn't want that to happen, so he stabbed her more than twenty times in the chest and the face."

I heard several women in the courtroom gasp. Mack Craig closed his eyes and shook his head and then continued, "I know it's hard for any of you to even imagine something so terrible happenin' here in our peaceful little town, but it certainly did, and on the day after Easter, no less. We'll show you pictures of the victim, and you'll see the knife he used to do the awful deed. Sittin' over there now, Jim Tressell may not look like a killer, but let me assure you that looks can be deceivin'. He's most definitely a killer. We have his fingerprints on the knife, and we found his fingerprints in the kitchen, the living room and the bedroom of the deceased."

He said the word "bedroom" like it was two long words.

"You will hear from people who saw him frequent the victim's home. Gentlemen, this is an open and shut case if there ever was one. I would be remiss if I didn't say thank you for your service on this jury, and thank you for your kind attention this morning."

He walked back to the table on the right side of the courtroom and sat down in a chair. He ran the fingers of his left hand through his hair which just messed it up some more.

I looked over at Mr. Tressell then. He was sitting on the left side of the courtroom at a wooden table next to his lawyer. He was looking down at the table even though there was nothing in front of him to see. He was wearing black pants and a white shirt with a collar. I'd never seen him wear anything but overalls. He looked older to me than he had when he'd been working in Miss Lucille's garden. I turned to look around the room for Mrs. Tressell, but I didn't see her. I whispered to ask Mama why she wasn't there. She whispered back that it was probably too hard for her to come and hear all of the bad things that would be said about Mr. Tressell.

The judge called on Rufus Cornelius then, and he stood up and walked over to face the jury. He was much younger than Mr. Craig. He had sandy brown hair that was parted and combed neatly to one side. He was wearing a blue suit and a red tie. Mama told me that the court had appointed him to serve as the attorney for Mr. Tressell. Daddy told her that this was Rufus Cornelius' first murder trial, but he should be good because he had graduated high up in his law school class at the University of Texas. Daddy said he also wrote articles for the law review. I didn't know what that meant, but it sounded like Daddy was impressed.

His voice didn't boom through the courtroom like Mr. Craig's did. It was much softer. I noticed that most of the people in the courtroom leaned forward when he started speaking just to be able to hear him.

"Thank you, Your Honor, and good morning gentlemen of the jury." He turned to face the twelve men in their jury box. "My name is Rufus Cornelius, and it's my responsibility to represent Mr. Jim Tressell in this very important case. The defendant stands here falsely accused of murder, a very serious crime. At the conclusion of this case we will ask for a verdict of not guilty. The burden of proof rests with the government in this case, and they have to prove beyond a reasonable doubt that the defendant is guilty. I assure you that they cannot do that because Jim Tressell would not and did not kill Lucille Harris. We will prove to you that there are numerous other people who could've killed Mrs. Harris. They had the motive and the opportunity. I'm confident that after you've heard all of the testimony and seen the evidence, you will vote to acquit the defendant in this case and let him return to his wife and his job at the railroad. Thank you." As he sat down at the table beside Mr. Tressell, he gave him a pat on his slumping right shoulder.

Judge Harper then told Mr. Craig to call his first witness.

"Your Honor, the people call Detective Albert Binotti to the stand," he said.

I was glad they were starting with Detective Binotti since I knew him and since I'd told him that Mr. Tressell would never hurt Miss Lucille. He came through the double doors at the back of the courtroom and walked straight to the chair that was up high on the right side of where the judge was sitting. He was wearing what he'd been wearing every time I'd seen him—khaki pants, a white shirt and cowboy boots. He wasn't wearing his cowboy hat. I knew that gentlemen didn't wear hats indoors. I had seen enough episodes of Perry Mason to know that he'd have to tell everyone his name, date of birth, his occupation and his place of residence. The judge asked him the questions which he answered. Then he put his hand on the Bible and swore to tell the whole truth and nothing but the truth.

The district attorney stood up and walked toward Detective Binotti.

"Would you please tell our distinguished jury and everyone in the courtroom how long you've been servin' the good people of Marshall as a detective?"

"I've been with the police force for twenty-seven years, and I've been a detective for the last eighteen."

"Sir, will you be so kind as to share with everyone the number of murder investigations that you've led?"

"Ten before this one."

"All in Marshall?"

"Yessir. We don't have a lot of murders here in Marshall as everyone here in the courtroom knows, but the ones we do have mostly involve someone gettin' drunk on the weekend and then pickin' an argument with a spouse or friend. Tempers flare, and a gun or a knife gets pulled, and someone ends up dead."

"That's truly a sad turn of events for the people involved, and when anyone gets killed in a fight, it's terrible. But I'm guessin' that you haven't had to investigate a murder quite like this one before where a pretty young woman has been so brutally murdered. Would I be right about that?"

"You're correct. I have not, and all of us in the department hope that we never have to again," he responded.

"Amen to that. Now let's get to that day when you were called to the scene of the murder. Can you take us through what happened the Monday after Easter this past April?"

"I can. We received a call at the station from Nita Rogers who is the closest neighbor to the victim. She said her daughter had come runnin' to their house yellin' about findin' the victim lyin' on her kitchen floor with blood on her blouse. The child had blood on her hands where she had tried to rouse the victim."

Some of the people in the courtroom turned to look at us. I looked down at my hands. They were shaking. Mama patted me on the arm and asked me if I wanted to leave. I shook my head from side to side.

"What time did that call come in to the station, Detective?"

"A few minutes after 4:00 PM. The child was a piano student of the victim's. She had gone next door and entered through the back door for her weekly piano lesson when she discovered the body."

"And what happened after that, Detective?"

"Officers Raymond Palmer and Joseph McKay drove to the scene on the corner of Rusk Street and Bishop. I followed them in my own squad car. Mrs. Rogers was waiting in the victim's front yard for us. She indicated that we should enter through the back door of Mrs. Harris' house which we did. We found the victim lyin' face down on the kitchen floor. There was a lot of blood around her head and upper body. I knelt down beside her and checked for a pulse. There wasn't one. I asked Officer Palmer to radio the department that we would need the Justice of the Peace to come to the scene. Then Officer McKay and I began to look more closely at the victim and the entire kitchen. There were yellow roses strewn around on the floor, and the bottom of what looked to be a broken flower vase was on the floor not far from the back door. That door led directly into the kitchen from the backyard. Pieces of glass were on the floor in front of and to the side of the victim. We later found pieces of glass under the ice box and even under the kitchen table. You know how when glass breaks, pieces can fly in all directions."

"Did you think at first that maybe Mrs. Harris could have fallen and hit her head?"

"That would have been a logical thought except there was so much blood on the floor around the victim. After I checked her pulse, I lifted one shoulder and saw that her entire blouse was covered with blood. I knew then that the blood couldn't have come from a fall. That amount of blood on and under someone's chest area indicated to me that she had been assaulted."

"After the Justice of the Peace arrived, were you able to determine exactly how Mrs. Lucille Harris had been killed?"

"Yes. She was stabbed over and over."

"Your Honor, I would like to submit into evidence photos that were taken of the victim at the scene. This won't be pleasant for the jury to see, but it's important they see how vicious this killin' was," Mr. Craig said as he turned to look at Mr. Tressell.

He gave a small stack of photos to a lady at the front of the courtroom. She took her time taping a tag with a number on it to the back of each photo. We all watched her as she worked. When she was finished with the last photo, she handed the small stack back to Mr. Craig. He looked at each one, shook his head and said to the jury, "Prepare yourselves. These are gruesome to see."

Everyone watched as the man at the end of the front row took the first picture Mr. Craig handed him. He looked at it quickly and passed it on. Nobody wanted to look at the photos very long. Some of the members of the jury frowned. Others shook their heads. Still others wiped sweat from their foreheads. Once all of the pictures had been passed to all twelve men, the last member of the jury handed the stack back to Mr. Craig.

"Gentleman, I think you'll agree with me that this was a terrible crime—a crime of passion—a crime by someone who was very upset with the victim, and that person must be held responsible for this awful crime," he was almost yelling now.

"Objection, Your Honor," said Mr. Cornelius. "He's givin' his closing argument."

"Sustained," said the judge.

Mr. Craig asked Detective Binotti to give more details about the crime scene and if he had searched the house for the murder weapon. He explained that he and the other officers had searched the kitchen first and then the entire house, but they hadn't found a bloody knife anywhere. Mr. Craig asked him if the murderer could have used one of the knives in the victim's own kitchen.

"We checked the kitchen drawers, and nothin' seemed out of place. The victim had only one knife that she most likely used for choppin' vegetables. The type of knife that was used in the killin' appeared to be much larger than her knife, and the knife in her drawer was clean. No blood on it, no blood in the drawer and no blood on the drawer handle. I've never found a murderer that would take time to wash off a weapon and then put it back in a drawer. They usually want to get away from the scene of the crime as fast as possible. They also take the weapon with 'em."

"And after all of your lookin' around the house, you did not find the murder weapon?"

"No sir. We didn't find it."

The judge interrupted Mr. Craig at that point and said that he thought it would be a good time to break for lunch and that court would resume at 2:00. When he stood up, we all stood and watched him walk out of the side door. Then it seemed to me that everyone started talking at one time. Mama took me by the hand and said it was time for us to leave.

"Are we comin' back after lunch?" I asked her when we were outside.

"I don't know if we should. Your daddy will not be the least bit happy with me for lettin' you hear all of that. He didn't think you should come at all."

"I know. If you don't think we should come back, it's okay. It's really hot in there, but I want to hear what else Detective Binotti has to say."

She gave me a hug then and said, "We'll see. Mavis is plannin' to keep Betsy all day, so let's get home and have some lunch after we cool off. Then we can decide."

⊷⊶

Mama made us ham sandwiches for lunch. After we finished them, she called Mavis who told her that Betsy was asleep, so we decided to go back to the courthouse for the afternoon session.

The judge asked Mr. Craig to continue. He called Detective Binotti back to the witness stand and asked him to tell the court if he had found anything else of interest at Miss Lucille's house.

"Well, the only other unusual thing we found was some perishable food sittin' out on the kitchen table. It was pretty obvious that Mrs. Harris had been to the grocery store before she was killed and hadn't had time to put her groceries away."

"Did you call local stores to ask if she had been shoppin' with them that mornin'?"

"We did. She had been down to Abraham's around 8:30 on that Monday morning. She didn't buy much—just a few items. Some ground beef, a head of lettuce, a carton of milk, some spaghetti and sauce, a few spices—so she was in and out of the store pretty quick."

"Did she indicate to anyone there at Abraham's that she was scared of anyone?"

"Not at all. Ted Abraham himself put her groceries in three small sacks so she could carry them inside easily when she got home. They both said she seemed happy and friendly as always. She shopped there quite a bit. We think she came home soon after she left Abraham's since two paper bags of groceries were still on the table. There was another bag with a box of spaghetti and a can of tomato sauce in the back seat of her car, and the car door had been left open."

"Was the car door open when you arrived?"

"No, sir. The neighbor child who found her closed it on her way to the back door—just being helpful."

"Do you think that the murderer was in the house when Mrs. Harris got home from the store?"

"It's possible, but not likely. If he had watched her leave, he wouldn't have known how long she would be gone. Also, a neighbor told us when we were askin' around that he saw a man wearin' dark clothes and a ball cap pulled low down on his head walkin' up the side street directly next to the victim's house around 9:00 AM. That's Bishop Street, and only her garden separates the side of her house from Bishop."

"Do you think this man in the dark clothes and cap could be the murderer?"

"We think it's likely given the estimated time of death."

"Who estimated the time of death? The Justice of the Peace?"

"No, sir. Our local JP, Cully Littlefield, as everyone here knows is part time in that job. He works at Haynes Feed Store and just comes out to pronounce someone dead. Since this was a murder, we called in the county medical examiner from over in Tyler to come do an autopsy."

"And the medical examiner from Tyler said that the time of death was when?"

"Between 8:00 and noon that day."

"So this man walkin' down Bishop Street could've seen her drive up and then come inside to murder Mrs. Harris. Is that correct?"

"Yessir. Mrs. Harris wasn't in the habit of lockin' her doors."

Detective Binotti explained that the man on Bishop probably saw Miss Lucille unloading the groceries from her car and followed her inside her house.

"And what do you believe happened then, Detective?"

Everyone in the jury box and in the courtroom seemed to lean forward to hear what was coming next.

"Shortly after she set the grocery sacks down on the table, she was attacked. Mrs. Harris never had time to take her groceries out of the sacks or go back to her car for the third sack. We think that her attacker handed her the vase with yellow roses. She most likely would've turned to set the vase on the kitchen counter and would've been at her most vulnerable then. That's when her attacker stabbed her. According to the report from the medical examiner, the first stab wound was in her back. She would've automatically dropped the vase on the floor which broke it into pieces and sent glass and roses flyin'."

The district attorney stopped then and asked the judge for permission to put a poster on an easel at the front of the courtroom. The poster showed an outline of a body standing up with its back to us.

Mr. Craig asked Detective Binotti to walk over to the easel, and he handed him a long thin stick. The detective used the stick to point out a place on the right side of Miss Lucille's back under her shoulder. He explained that that this was where the first stab wound was and that according to the medical examiner, it was a pretty deep wound but not deadly. He said that Miss Lucille would've most likely turned around to face her attacker after that first stabbing.

"And what do you think happened next?"

"The victim tried to fend off her attacker. She had cut wounds on her arms."

Detective Binotti pointed to both of the forearms on the poster.

"Anywhere else?" asked Mr. Craig.

"On her hands, too. It looked like she was protectin' both her face and upper body which would be a natural reaction if you were bein' attacked with a knife."

When Detective Binotti was back on the witness stand, Mr. Craig continued.

"Does it appear that the victim fell face down on her kitchen floor?"

"No. It doesn't. It looked like Mrs. Harris had been stabbed several times in the chest while she was standing up and then even more times than that after she fell onto her back. One of the chest wounds killed her, and once she was deceased, her attacker continued to stab her in the chest and then in the face."

"Twenty times, I believe. Is that correct?"

"Actually twenty-two stab wounds were found by the medical examiner. That includes the cuts on her face."

"I believe I remember you sayin' that you found her face down. Is that correct?"

"Yessir. Face down on the kitchen floor."

"How did she end up face down if she was mainly stabbed on her arms and in her chest and face?"

"We think that the killer turned her over when he was through stabbin' her. There were two yellow roses found under the middle part of her body. We think that the killer placed those roses under the body since the other ten roses were closer to the back door."

A woman sitting across the aisle from us in the courtroom appeared to faint and had to be helped out by the guard who was standing by the back door.

"Why would the killer place two roses underneath her body?"

"That's one question we haven't been able to answer, Mr. Craig."

"Why do you suppose he'd turn her over?"

"Maybe he was sorry for what he'd done and couldn't look at her or maybe he was tryin' to punish her even more by pushin' her face into the floor."

Before Mr. Craig could ask another question, the judge looked at his watch and said, "It's almost 4:00 o'clock. Let's wrap it up for today and start again at 9:00 tomorrow morning." He hit his gavel on the desk and said, "Court is adjourned." When he stood up, we all stood, too. Mama grabbed my hand, and we left the courtroom. As we reached the bottom of the concrete steps on the outside of the courthouse, I heard someone calling my name.

"Bobbi!" The voice sounded like a girl's, but when Mama and I turned around, I saw that it was Harry Price. He was carrying a shoe box and came over to us.

"Hey, Harry," I said. "This is my mama."

"Nita Rogers," said Mama. "I don't think we've met, but you know my husband, Coach Rogers."

"I sure do. I sold him a pair of black Florsheim brogues with rounded toes," Harry told her. "To wear to church. All leather soles and heels. I recommended that he take them to Brown's Leather Shop to have them add taps to the toes and heels. That would make them last twenty-five years, but he told me that he didn't like makin' noise when he walked."

"How'd you remember all that?" I asked him.

"I know all about the best kind of wood to use for the lasts in shoes, too. It's maple. That's what makes me a good shoe sales-man. I know all about shoes, and I remember what I sell to ev-erybody, so when they come back in, I can sell them somethin' different. Y'all been to the trial?"

I nodded yes, and Mama answered, "Mornin' and afternoon. It's so hot in there and not easy to listen to the terrible things that happened either."

"I can't imagine why you wanna hear it since you already know all about it."

"She was our friend and Bobbi's piano teacher, too."

"I know that, but everyone knows he did it. Doesn't seem to be a need to even have a trial if you ask me," he said.

"He didn't kill her."

"Settle down there, little girl. No need to get mad at me. He's the one you should be mad at. I saw him walkin' on Bishop that mornin'. I'm gonna be called as a witness."

I started to cry then. Mama put her arm around my shoulders. Other people were looking our way.

"We better be headin' home now, Harry."

"Didn't mean to make you cry," he said. "I know you think good of him. I wish I hadn't seen so much. Better go, too. I gotta deliver these shoes to a man over at Naders and then get back to work at the Hub." He waved as he turned away from us.

"I'm sorry he upset you," Mama said as we walked in front of our church and turned right to head down Rusk Street. "I think most people have already made up their minds about Mr. Tressell."

I started crying again. "I just know he wouldn't hurt her. He was always so nice to her."

"It's possible that he did, Bobbi, that maybe somethin' snapped inside him. Maybe he didn't want to hear that she was breakin' up with him."

"You think he was her boyfriend like people are sayin'?"

"I think maybe he was. He spent so much time with her in her garden and would go inside her house with her. That's really not proper for a married man to do with a young widow lady like Miss Lucille. And even you said you saw them kissin' one time."

"I know I did, but you said they were just friends."

"That's what I thought, but the signs don't look good."

"What signs?"

"Well, the kind of signs that point to bein' more than friends. Some of the other neighbors have been tellin' me things they saw goin' on at her house."

"You mean like the colored boys and girls singin' and playin' the piano?" I asked.

"Not that. There was plenty of talk about that, too, but this was more about Mr. Tressell spendin' too much time with her and not enough time with his wife. That's not a good thing for a marriage, Bobbi. You remember that when you get married."

"Daddy's gone a lot from us."

"He is, but he's at the field house with other men and with his football boys. He's not helpin' a young woman with her garden. That can lead to problems. Do you understand what I'm tellin' you?"

"I think so, but I still can't see why he would hurt her."

"I can't either, but it sure looks like he did."

───◄┤ ├►───

On Tuesday morning Mama and I once again dropped off Betsy with Mavis and started walking toward town. We didn't see Mrs. Tressell, but I figured that she was inside since her front door was closed and her blinds were drawn over her front windows.

"You think that Mrs. Tressell will come to the trial at all?" I asked Mama.

"I really doubt it, Bobbi. It must be upsettin' for her to know people think he was Miss Lucille's boyfriend and that he's a killer. It's also hard for her to get around, I imagine."

"The courthouse has an elevator. I saw it yesterday."

"I know, but someone would have to carry her up the outside steps in her wheelchair to get to the main floor so that she could take the elevator to the second floor. She's never been one to wanna be around people. She's never even come to our picnics."

"I know. The picnic last summer was when Miss Lucille met Mr. Tressell. I sat at the table with them."

"I remember you did."

"That's when he invited her to see his garden. I wish she'd never gone or even come to the picnic. Then she'd be alive now."

"It's always easy to look back and wish to change things. I agree this is certainly one of those things we would all change if we could."

We reached the courthouse and lined up outside with a crowd of people. Most of them I recognized from the day before. When they opened the big double doors, we all filed in and took our places on the benches in the courtroom. It was already hot inside, and I was sweaty from our walk to town.

When Detective Binotti came in and took his place on the witness stand again, he was dressed just the same as he had been the day before.

"Good morning, Detective. Let me remind you that you're still under oath," the judge told him. "Mr. Craig, please continue."

"Detective, you said that you searched the house lookin' for the murder weapon. Is that correct?"

"We looked in every room—under the furniture, in drawers, even under the mattress on the bed. We also looked all around the house and in the garden."

"Did you look in her garage?"

"We did. She had a one car garage that was separate from the house. We searched it, too. We found some gardenin' tools but no knife."

"But did you eventually find the knife that was used in the murder?"

"We did, or to be accurate, I should say some neighborhood children found it for us."

"And where did they find it?"

"The same child that discovered Mrs. Harris' body found the knife hidden under a feed sack in Mr. Philip Baxter's chicken house. Mr. Baxter lives on Rusk Street next door to the defendant."

Mr. Craig asked the judge for permission to put another poster on the easel. It was a map of our neighborhood. He pointed out where everyone lived on Rusk Street and how close Mr. Tressell's house was to Tada's chicken house. He showed the jury that Miss Lucille's house was at the corner of Rusk and Bishop. He explained about our game of hide 'n seek and how I found the knife in the chicken house. He said that we only touched the dish towel, not the knife and then we took the knife to Mama.

When he said Mama's name, a number of people in the courtroom turned to look at us. I looked straight ahead at Detective Binotti hoping that he would keep talking so that people wouldn't stare at us.

Mr. Craig asked him what he did next, and he said they sent the knife to Tyler to be examined for fingerprints and then they started interviewing people they knew had been in contact with Miss Lucille or had a close relationship to her.

I noticed that Mr. Tressell never seemed to move. He just sat at the table with his head facing the judge. He didn't turn his head from side to side or even seem to move it to look at Detective Binotti when he was talking.

"Did you question the defendant after the knife was found?" Mr. Craig asked.

"Yessir. Officer Palmer drove with me to the home of the defendant. This was the second time we had been there to question him."

"So he was already a suspect?"

"We'd been told that he had a close relationship with the deceased. As I said we were talking to anyone who knew her well. She had lived in Marshall a little over nine months, but as a teacher at Bishop College and as a member of First Baptist Church, she knew a number of people."

"Did you interview all of them?"

"Only the ones that would've had a reason to kill her."

No one in the courtroom was moving.

"So you'd determined that the defendant had a reason to kill Mrs. Harris. Is that correct?"

"He had a motive. Yes."

"What was that motive?"

"They had been romantically involved, and the victim had broken up with him."

"But isn't he a married man?"

"That's correct. He's married."

"Did you ask the defendant if he had been romantically involved with the victim?"

"Yessir, I did, but he wouldn't answer that question. We also asked him where he was during the four hour period on the day of the murder when the medical examiner said that Mrs. Harris had been killed, and he told us he'd been asleep. He works the night shift, 11-7 at the railroad, or he did."

"Are you tellin' the members of the jury that his alibi was that he was asleep?"

"Yessir. That's what he told us."

"Could anyone corroborate that?"

"His wife was at home, but she was asleep on the couch in their front room when he got home from work. She didn't hear him come in or see him asleep in his bed until she woke up about 11:30 that mornin'. Seems she felt ill in the night, took some pain medicine and fell asleep on the couch."

"Did she normally hear her husband when he came in from work?"

"She said she did because she was usually asleep in their bedroom, but this time she wasn't in there."

"So he could've come home, gotten the knife, gone to the victim's house, murdered her and then come back to his house and climbed in his bed all before his wife woke up."

"Objection," Mr. Cornelius said as he stood. "He's leading the witness."

"Sustained. Put it in the form of a question, Mr. Craig."

"Yes, Your Honor."

"Based on your experience would you say that Jim Tressell had time to come home after his shift ended at the railroad at 7:00 in the mornin', get the knife, kill Mrs. Harris and come back to his house before his wife woke up around 11:30?"

"Yessir. He did."

Judge Harper spoke up then and said, "Counselor, this is a good time to recess for lunch. We'll resume at 2:00."

He stood up. We did, too. It seemed that everyone in the courtroom started to talk then.

Mama and I waited until most of the people had left the courtroom before we stood up. She wanted to speak to Miss Lucille's brother since we hadn't had the chance to do that yesterday. When he and Miss Patty stood up and turned toward the back of the courtroom, she waved to them. He waved back, and they walked toward us. He looked so much like Miss Lucille that it was almost like she was walking over to say hello to us.

"This has been quite a morning," he said. "I still have a hard time believin' that the man sittin' at the table over there would kill my sister. He doesn't look like a killer."

"Larry," said Miss Patty and nodded my way.

"Patty, the child's at the trial. I'm not saying anything she hasn't heard already."

"I know that some people are prob'ly sayin' I shouldn't let Bobbi come here, but she and Lucille were so close, and she wants to be here," Mama said. "To tell you the truth, it's a comfort to me to have her beside me. I like keepin' her close these days. This whole thing has been so hard on all of us, and I can't even imagine how hard it must be for the two of you."

"We just want justice for her. If he killed her, he deserves what's comin' to him. From what all the detective has told us, it looks like he did it."

I felt really sad then and pulled on Mama's hand.

Larry looked down at me and asked, "Are you enjoyin' Lucille's piano? Still takin' lessons and all?"

"Yessir. Mama found me a new teacher. She's nice but not as nice as Miss Lucille. She's doesn't smile very much, but she has contests for us to see who practices the most, so I'm tryin' hard to win."

"I'm glad her piano found a good home with you." He wiped his eyes then, and Miss Patty patted him on the arm.

Mama said, "We better let you get some lunch since the trial'll start up again at 2:00."

"We're really not very hungry, but we're goin' over to Woolworth's to grab a bite. Care to join us?"

"Thank you, but we better head home for our lunch. I need to check on my other daughter. She's across the street at the Baxters' house."

"The house with the chicken coop in back?"

She nodded.

"Bobbi, thank you for finding the knife in there," he said as they turned to leave the courtroom.

"Mama, I wish I hadn't found it."

"I know, honey, but somebody would've found it eventually. If Jim Tressell killed her, it's best that he go on trial and face his punishment for doin' somethin' so terrible. Let's get on home."

Mama called Mavis to ask about Betsy. She assured her that Betsy was fine. Katie was entertaining Annie and Betsy by pretending to be their art teacher. Mavis said that Katie missed me.

"I know you miss playin' with Katie and Law, but it's too hot for you to be outside all afternoon anyway." I knew what she meant because we were both patting our faces with tissues as we took our places on the back row in the courtroom. Everyone seemed to sit in the same places like assigned seats at my school.

When Detective Binotti was on the witness stand again, Mr. Craig asked, "Detective, since there was so much blood around the victim and in her kitchen, wouldn't that mean that the attacker would've gotten blood on his clothes?"

"Yessir. There's no way to stab someone twenty-two times and not get blood on your clothes."

"Did you find any bloody clothes in the defendant's home?"

"No, sir. We searched his home, but between the time of the murder and when we first went to his house to question him, he would've had plenty of time to discard the clothin'," said the detective. "He also has a burn bin at the back of his garden, so it would've been easy to get rid of the bloody clothes in there."

"Did you also search the chicken house?"

"We did."

Mr. Craig then said to the judge, "I would like to enter the knife that was found in the chicken house into evidence." After the knife was tagged, he held it up for the jury to see. Then he turned to Detective Binotti and asked him to explain why he thought this was the knife that had been used to kill Miss Lucille. He told the jury about the knife being a Cutco and how Cutco was engraved on the blade. He also explained that Cutco knives are only sold by door-to-door salesmen and have a reputation for being very sharp. He told about one Cutco salesman who cut his own finger when he was demonstrating a knife for a customer. A few people chuckled when he said that the salesman ended up having to go to the hospital because the knife was so sharp.

"When you were at the home of the defendant, did you ask him if he owned a Cutco knife?"

"I did, and he said he and his wife owned two Cutco knives. He said they bought them last fall since they cut up so many vegetables from his garden."

"Did you ask him to show you the knives when you went to his home?"

"I did. He went to the kitchen and brought back one knife. It was a Cutco. When I asked him if he could bring me the second knife, he told me it wasn't in the kitchen. He said he didn't know where it might be, that he or Mrs. Tressell must have misplaced it."

"He said that they must have misplaced an expensive knife like that?"

"That's what he told us. He didn't have any other explanation."

"Did he ask his wife if she knew where the knife might be?"

"She was restin' when we were there—back in the bedroom. I thought it was better not to ask him to get her up while we were questionin' him about the murder. He was not much of a talker to begin with."

"Did the knife ever turn up at their home?"

"No, sir. It couldn't have turned up because we had sent the knife to the medical examiner over in Tyler."

The crowd started to whisper. The judge asked for order.

"Detective Binotti, in your esteemed opinion, is the person who killed Mrs. Lucille Harris in the courtroom today?" Mr. Craig asked.

"Yessir. Based on the evidence, Jim Tressell murdered Mrs. Harris the day after Easter."

"No further questions for this witness, Your Honor," said Mr. Craig. "But I do reserve the right to redirect after cross examination."

Judge Harper nodded and said, "Mr. Cornelius, your witness."

Mr. Cornelius stood up and walked over in front of Detective Binotti.

"Detective, you've been answerin' a lot of questions. Do you need a glass of water before we continue?" he asked as he smiled at

Detective Binotti. I knew from watching Perry Mason on television that he was just trying to be friendly and make a good impression on the jury.

Everything Daddy had heard about Mr. Cornelius was good. He was supposed to be very smart, and people said that he was always prepared for his trials, but this was his first murder trial. Perry Mason had been in a lot of trials and knew just what questions to ask the witness. Juries always seemed to like Perry Mason. Mr. Cornelius looked a lot younger than Mr. Craig and Perry Mason. He was wearing black round glasses and a navy blue suit and a red tie which made him look very patriotic. As he walked toward Detective Binotti, he cocked his head to one side like he was thinking about something.

"I would like for us to talk a little bit about the neighborhood where Mrs. Harris lived. I believe you were familiar with Rusk Street and the neighbors who live there before this incident. Is that correct?"

"Yessir."

"Could you please tell everyone here in Judge Harper's courtroom why you were called in your official capacity to Rusk Street back in June of last year?"

"The police department received a call that there had been a Peepin' Tom in the neighborhood. He had been lookin' in the bedroom of Lottie Van Worth who lives on Rusk Street."

Mr. Cornelius asked the judge for permission to put a map of Rusk Street on the easel. Then he asked the detective to point out where the Peepin' Tom had been seen.

"It appears to me that the Peepin' Tom was reported to be at a house just two doors down from Mrs. Harris' house. Would you agree with that assessment?" Mr. Cornelius asked.

"That's correct. The houses are on the same side of Rusk Street."

"Would I also be correct in assuming that you apprehended the Peepin' Tom, so it was impossible for him to be considered as a suspect in this murder?"

"No, sir."

"So you're saying that a man who was looking in the window of neighbor who lived close to Mrs. Harris was never arrested. He was never even identified?"

"We followed a number of leads, but we didn't find him."

"Would it seem possible to you that a man who would look in a lady's window might be emboldened to do more than that when he realized that a young widow lady had moved into a neighborhood that was known for not keeping their doors locked?"

"We had no reason to believe that a Peepin' Tom's next step would be murder, and the murder was months after the report of a man peepin' in a window," responded the detective.

"But you agree that this Peepin' Tom had been to Rusk Street and had committed a crime there once before?"

"I agree, but we think that they were different people."

"But you cannot be absolutely sure of that."

"Anything's possible."

"Looking again at this map of the neighborhood, I'm realizing just how close Bishop College is to Mrs. Harris' home. It's just across Rusk and Bishop Streets—maybe not even a five minute walk. Mrs. Harris was a teacher there. Is that correct?"

"Yessir. That's been reported in the newspapers, so everyone knows that she was a teacher at Bishop."

"I didn't know Mrs. Harris, but from what people have told me, she was a very pretty lady. I've been told that some of Mrs. Harris' students from Bishop visited her home on occasion in the evening, so they would've known her well enough to know that she didn't lock her doors. Detective, did you consider during your investigation that one of the colored boys from Bishop might've developed a crush on his pretty music teacher? He might've decided that he wanted to get to know her better, so he paid her a visit the morning of the murder. Did you even consider that any of her colored students at Bishop College could've committed this crime?"

"We questioned several of the colored boys from the college. Three had been to her home on Halloween, and she had five other boys come to her house during the school year to practice for programs at the college. We questioned all of them."

"And none of them could have committed this murder?"

"They all had alibis. Most of the students were away from the college for Easter break and didn't return to the school until Monday afternoon—hours after the murder took place. The boys we questioned were on their way back to school from their hometowns, so they weren't even in Marshall."

"Would I be correct in saying that some of these boys gave each other alibis? That they were supposedly in a car together?"

"That's correct."

"Could some of them have gotten together and come up with an alibi for one of their friends?"

"I guess that's possible, but we questioned them pretty hard. I think at least one of 'em would've broken down and told us the truth if they'd made up a lie like that."

"How many colored boys attend Bishop College, Detective?"

"Two hundred and ten."

"Did you question all two hundred ten?"

"No, sir. We questioned only the boys who knew the victim."

"But any of these male students could've seen this pretty teacher going into her home which was less than five minutes from the school. Would you agree?"

"You can't keep someone from watchin' as you enter your home, but we did find a knife with the defendant's fingerprints on it," stated the detective.

"Please stick to answerin' the questions," said the judge.

"Since you brought up that knife, let's talk about it, sir. Who determined my client's fingerprints were on the knife?"

"The medical examiner from Tyler did. He will be takin' the stand later. You can ask him yourself."

"No need to get testy, sir. I'm just trying to understand about this knife. Were there any other fingerprints on the knife? Did you check the fingerprints of any of the other men who live on Rusk Street or the boys from Bishop you questioned?"

"We didn't have him check for other fingerprints. Those people you named didn't have a motive."

"I'm trying to figure out if everyone who touched this knife treated it with kid gloves so that you could be absolutely sure that only Mr. Tressell had his fingerprints on it. But what you're telling me is that someone else could've touched the knife and actually used it to kill Mrs. Harris, but you wouldn't know that because you only checked for my client's fingerprints. Am I right about that?"

"It doesn't matter if anyone else touched the knife. Your client used that knife to kill Mrs. Harris!"

Before Mr. Cornelius could ask another question, the judge interrupted and said that he was adjourning court for the day. He stood up, and so did we. The jury left the courtroom, and the talk started again.

On the way home I asked Mama why Detective Binotti had gotten so upset, and she told me that he was probably tired from all the questions over two days. He had investigated the murder and believed he knew what happened. Mr. Cornelius was just trying to put reasonable doubt in the mind of the jurors like Perry Mason did. He wanted them to think that it was possible that someone else could have killed Miss Lucille.

"Isn't it possible, Mama?"

"Of course, it's possible. A man is innocent until proven guilty. That's what the trial is about."

"Mr. Cornelius wants the men on the jury to believe that the Peepin' Tom or one of Lucille's students or even another boy from the college could've been her attacker. All of the evidence so far has pointed to Mr. Tressell. He's tryin' to point it toward other places."

"They never caught the Peepin' Tom. You remember when I told you about the boy sackin' groceries at Abraham's havin' bug eyes?"

"I remember."

"I saw him again at the sit-in at the courthouse. He was there yellin' bad words at the colored kids."

"You know I don't agree with what he did at the sit-in, but that doesn't make him the Peepin' Tom or a murderer."

"But somebody else could've hurt Miss Lucille. That's what Mr. Cornelius was sayin', right?"

"That's what he's sayin'."

That night at dinner, Daddy asked Mama what had happened at the trial. She told him about Detective Binotti's testimony. She also told him that Mr. Cornelius seemed like a smart young man who had a nice smile. Daddy asked me if I'd been having bad dreams, and I told him no. I told him I was learning a lot at the trial but that it was a lot slower moving than Perry Mason was. He laughed when I said that and told me that he thought that most judges, lawyers and juries would like trials to be more like Perry Mason and be over in an hour.

"How long do people say the trial might last?" he asked Mama.

"I've been hearin' some of the people say maybe another week. Nobody knows how many witnesses will be called, but the detective's the main one. He knows the most, I think."

"He's done all the investigatin'. He's a good man and has had a lot of experience testifyin' at trials. Are you girls goin' to all of it?"

"That will depend on Mavis. I feel bad askin' her to keep Betsy so much, but she doesn't seem to mind. If it gets to be too much for her, we'll stay home."

"And what about you, Bobbi girl? Are you tired of sittin' in a hot courtroom all day?"

"It's not really all day, Daddy. We get to come home for lunch, and the judge lets us out at 4:00."

"That's pretty much all day to me, but it's good I get to hear all about it straight from the horse's mouth."

Mama and I both laughed when it sounded like he was calling us horses.

"You're too much, Jack Rogers! Why don't you tell me all about football practice after I get the girls bathed and into bed?"

"I'll do it," he said and winked at her.

Detective Binotti was back on the stand the next morning when the trial started up again at 9:00. He didn't look as tired as he had the day before.

"I just have a couple more questions about the knife, detective, and then we'll move on. Could anyone else have touched the knife?"

"Of course, someone else could've touched the knife before it was used in the murder."

"The children who found it?"

"They said they didn't touch it."

I looked at Mama and shook my head no.

"But can you be sure? Did they know to hold it just so like it was evidence in a murder?" He held up a pencil carefully between his two pointer fingers.

"They didn't know that it was evidence, and I cannot guarantee how they held it, but they told me they didn't touch it. They only touched the dish towel it was wrapped in."

"Did Mr. Tressell keep his doors locked all the time?"

That question seemed to surprise the detective.

"I didn't ask him that."

"Is it conceivable that someone could've come into the house, stolen the knife and then used it to kill Mrs. Harris? My client's fingerprints would've been on the knife just from regular kitchen use."

"It's highly unlikely that someone stole the knife from Mr. Tressell's kitchen since his wife's at home all the time. She's in a wheelchair and doesn't leave home much from what I've been told."

"But if he didn't lock the doors, and they both happened to be gone at the same time, could someone have entered the home and stolen the knife?"

"Yessir."

"I've been thinking about the knife and the chicken house. Why would someone murder another human being and then not do a better job of hiding the murder weapon?"

"I don't have an answer to that."

"Let's say that you were Jim Tressell and you had a big garden in your backyard. You're a strong man. Couldn't you have just pushed that knife deep into the garden somewhere? No one would ever find it."

"Objection," called out Mr. Craig. "Is he making up fairy tales now, Your Honor?"

"Sustained. What is the question, Mr. Cornelius?"

"Would you have hidden a bloody knife in a chicken house in your own neighborhood? Why wouldn't he have taken it to work at the railroad and put it on a train and sent it far away from here?"

"I agree it wasn't a good place to hide the knife, but he was in a hurry. He killed her and then knew he had to hurry home, dispose of the knife and his clothes and get into bed before his wife woke up."

"You testified that you never found the bloody clothes. Wasn't that what you said?"

"We didn't find the clothes he was wearin'."

"Well, it just seems strange to me that the murderer wouldn't get rid of the knife when he got rid of the clothes, but let's talk about the yellow roses now. Why do you suppose yellow roses were at the scene of the crime?"

"We believe he sent them to her or took them when he went to her house."

"As what, a gift? I came to kill you, but I wanted to give you some roses first?" Mr. Cornelius turned to look at the jury then.

"He'd sent her roses once before."

"And when was this?"

"On her birthday in November."

"I believe that someone sent her roses, but the card was signed 'From a Secret Admirer.'"

"According to Mary Ross at Rainbow Floral, Jim Tressell bought yellow roses in November and paid cash for them. One of her neighbors was at her home when the roses were delivered and saw the card that had Secret Admirer on it. He sent roses to her then and sent some more yellow roses around Easter."

"Did he pay cash for the second order of roses?"

"Paid with a check. Mrs. Ross said that he wanted to pay cash, but roses had gone up in price a dollar, and he didn't have enough money with him. He wrote a check. That's how she knew his name."

"I'd like to go back to earlier in your testimony, Detective Binotti, if I may. Yesterday you said that there were a couple of ways that the attacker could've gotten into the home of Mrs. Harris. Is that correct?"

"It's impossible to know since there were no witnesses to the crime."

"I thank you for pointing that out to all of us. It's much easier to be absolutely sure that you have the right person when you have a witness. Isn't that right?"

"It's always best to have a witness."

"And I believe you told us that you've never had to investigate a crime quite like this one. Isn't that what you said?"

"I said I've investigated a number of murders. None of them were this bloody."

"So even though you've not had experience with this particular type of crime and you admit that you don't have a witness, you still feel qualified to decide who committed this murder?"

"Yessir. Based on the evidence."

"And that evidence being a knife that was found in a chicken house that could've been touched by any number of people or could've been stolen from the kitchen of Jim Tressell who's never been in any trouble before in his life? That's good enough for you to want to send this man to the electric chair?"

He turned and pointed at Mr. Tressell who flinched when he said the words "electric chair."

"You said earlier in your testimony it was possible that the attacker brought the roses with him to her house, but now you're saying that they were delivered. Which one is it?"

"We can't really say. The delivery man was temporary help at the florist over the busy Easter weekend. He no longer lives in Marshall. He moved away shortly after Easter."

"Did you consider the delivery man to be a suspect?"

"No."

"Even though he could've delivered the roses, gone into her house and then killed Mrs. Harris? How convenient that he moved away from Marshall."

"He was a young man. Very slight of build. He wasn't strong enough to tangle with a woman in good shape like Mrs. Harris. He hadn't worked at Rainbow Floral long. And what motive would he have to kill a woman he was deliverin' flowers to?"

"I'm supposed to ask the questions." Mr. Cornelius turned away from Detective Binotti and walked back toward his table. He looked at some papers on the table, and then said, "No further questions, Your Honor."

Detective Binotti got up slowly from the witness stand and walked out the back door of the courtroom. He was shaking his head from side to side as he left. Mr. Craig's next witness was Waylon Hutto, Medical Examiner for the East Texas District based in Tyler. He put his hand on the Bible and promised to tell the truth just like Detective Binotti had done.

Mr. Hutto was wearing a dark suit and a polka dotted bow tie. He had on gold glasses that looked too big for his face. He didn't have much hair. Daddy would call it a buzz cut.

Mr. Craig put his posters showing the body and the stab wounds back on the easel. Mr. Hutto pointed out that the first stab wound was on the upper right part of her back under her shoulder blade and was about one inch deep. He said that it would have hurt but would not have been fatal. Mr. Hutto came down from the witness stand to point out the locations of the next nine stab wounds which were mainly cuts on the forearms and hands where Miss Lucille was trying to defend herself.

"And what about the other twelve stab wounds?"

"One of the next wounds was in her chest and was the one that most likely knocked her down. It was here in the middle of her chest." He used the pointer again. "She would have bled a lot from that one because it severed an artery. Once she was on the floor, the attacker then stabbed her seven more times in the chest. She died from one of those wounds—right above her heart."

The courtroom was very quiet. I saw some of the men on the jury look at Mr. Tressell. He was looking down at the table in front of him.

"If I've counted right, that still leaves us with four more wounds. Is that correct, Mr. Hutto?"

"Yes, sir. The last four wounds came after she was dead and before she was turned onto her stomach. The attacker cut X marks across both of her cheeks here and here." He pointed to both sides of the face on the poster.

Several women gasped. This was the first time that any of us had heard about the X marks.

"That sounds mighty gruesome. Were these deep wounds, Mr. Hutto?"

"Superficial cuts across both cheeks. Seemed to me to be some sort of sign the attacker was leaving on her."

"No further questions, Your Honor."

As Mr. Hutto was making his way back to the witness stand, I saw Mr. Tressell lean over to tell Mr. Cornelius something. This was the first time Mr. Tressell had said anything to his lawyer during the trial.

When they finished talking, Mr. Cornelius stood up and said, "Good morning, Mr. Hutto. I have just a couple of questions for you. In your expert opinion, do you think that the attacker was stronger than Mrs. Harris?"

"Yes, sir. I believe that he had to be stronger to subdue the victim like he did. She was fighting for her life and was a young, healthy woman."

"If her attacker was a strong man like my client, wouldn't you expect the wounds to be deep ones?"

"That's hard to say."

"How deep was the chest wound you said most likely would've knocked Mrs. Harris to the floor?"

"Three inches."

"Were any of the other wounds deeper than three inches?

"No, sir."

"Looking at my client over there, wouldn't you think that he would be able with a sharp Cutco knife in his hand to stab a woman deeper than three inches?"

"He appears to be a strong man."

"With those muscled up arms of his, I think he could stab someone clean through if he wanted to." Mr. Cornelius slammed his hand down hard on the table where Mr. Tressell was sitting. We all jumped. "What do you think, Mr. Hutto?"

Startled, Mr. Hutto said, "You make a good point."

"No further questions, Your Honor."

"You may step down, Mr. Hutto. We'll recess until 2:00."

❧ ☙

When court resumed for the afternoon, Mama and I were both a little surprised to see Mr. Tressell talking again to Mr. Cornelius as they sat at their table together. It seemed like he had finally realized he was on trial for murder.

Mr. Craig called his next witness—Harry Price.

Harry came walking in from the back. He was wearing a short–sleeved shirt, black trousers, a solid navy tie and shiny black loafers. He walked on his toes down the aisle to the stand—walking the same way and dressed the same way as every time I had seen him on Rusk Street walking to and from work.

"My name's Harry Price. I was born on June 21, 1936, and I sell shoes over at the Hub Shoe Store here in Marshall. I can sell you a new pair, Mr. Craig, if you come by to see me. It looks like you could use a new pair of shoes."

Everyone leaned forward trying to look at Mr. Craig's shoes. Some people in the courtroom and even a few men on the jury laughed. After he promised to tell the truth, Harry looked up and saw me in the back of the courtroom.

"Hey there, Bobbi," he called out as he waved to me. I gave a little wave back. "I told you and your mama that I was gonna be a witness. Here I am."

"This is a trial, Mr. Price," the judge told Harry. "It's not the Christmas parade."

"I know it's a trial, Judge Harper. It's just that I saw Bobbi back there at the back of the courtroom. She's my friend. I met her the day of the sit-in here at the courthouse. When I heard about the

163

murder, I was sure one of those colored boys from the sit-in had killed that pretty lady."

"The jury will disregard that last comment," said the judge. "Mr. Craig, get control of your witness, or I will hold him in contempt."

"Is that bad?" Harry asked. "I've never been to a trial before."

"It's very bad, so unless you want to end up in jail yourself, settle down and just answer the questions Mr. Craig asks you," Judge Harper said raising his voice.

"I'm ready," Harry said to Mr. Craig.

"Can you tell us what you were doin' on the mornin' of Monday, April 3rd of this year? That was the mornin' after Easter Sunday."

"That mornin' I got myself dressed, shined my shoes and ate my breakfast at my house."

"Can you tell us where you live?"

"Over on Oak Street. It's a dirt road right off of Rusk Street near Bishop College."

"Do you usually walk down Rusk Street to your job in downtown?"

"Yessir. I walk that way every day of the week except Sunday when we're closed at the Hub."

"What time of day do you usually pass by the house where Mrs. Lucille Harris lived?"

"A little before 9:00 in the mornin'. I have to be at work by 9:30, and I like to get there early so that I can cool off a little bit before my first customer comes in. I sweat a lot. You can see that from the rings under my arms." He held up his arms for everyone to see the wet places.

"We're all a little wet on this hot August day. On this particular day, the mornin' after Easter, did you happen to notice anyone else out walkin' on Rusk Street?"

"I didn't see anybody else on Rusk Street, but I did see a man walkin' my way on Bishop Street. I looked over there to see if it was anybody I knew."

"Did you know this man?"

"I can't say for sure. He was wearin' dark trousers, a dark coat and a ball cap pulled down low over his face. He also had on scuffed work boots. I always notice a man's shoes." Harry seemed proud about that.

"Could you tell what color this man was?"

"No, sir. I couldn't because he was also wearin' gloves. That seemed really strange to me because it wasn't cold that mornin'."

"Did he come all the way to Rusk Street where you were?"

"No, sir. He didn't keep walkin' toward me. He turned off of Bishop into the driveway behind Mrs. Harris' house."

"Could this person you saw that mornin' on Bishop have been the defendant Jim Tressell?"

"Yessir. He could've been Jim Tressell."

"Do you think that it's likely that you saw the man who murdered Mrs. Harris turn off of Bishop and go into Mrs. Harris' backyard?"

No one was moving.

"I think I did, but I didn't know it at the time."

"Had you ever seen a man go into her backyard before?"

"I'd seen Jim Tressell workin' in her garden before. I even saw them smoochin' out there a time or two, so I didn't think anything about somebody goin' into her backyard. For all I knew she had more than one boyfriend. He seemed too old for her to me."

"Just answer the questions, Mr. Price. We don't need your commentary," said the judge.

"How tall would you say this man was—the man you saw the mornin' of April 3rd?"

"I can't be sure, but he looked to be about my height. I'm 5 feet 10 inches in my loafers. I can get to six feet when I wear my Ports ankle boots that have little heels."

A few people chuckled.

Judge Harper looked their way.

"No further questions," said Mr. Craig.

"Your witness, Counselor."

"Mr. Price, was this man you saw that mornin' the same height as Mr. Tressell?"

"I said it could've been him."

"How tall do you think I am, Mr. Price?"

"You look to be about my height, and you're wearing Florsheim oxfords, so I'd say 5 feet 10 inches."

"Would you be surprised if I told you that I'm 6 feet 1 inch tall?"

"Yessir, I would."

"Should we infer from your answer that you think all men are about your height—5 feet 10 inches?"

I heard more laughter.

"I don't think that's right. Some people are shorter than me. Some are taller."

"You told us that the man you saw that mornin' was about your height, and you said I was about your height. Do you really have any idea how tall the man was?"

"Well, I wasn't that close to him, so it's hard to say."

"Mr. Price, you mentioned when you first took the stand that you thought a colored boy might have killed Mrs. Harris? What made you think that?" Mr. Cornelius asked him.

"Well, she taught at a colored college, she knew a lot of colored boys, and we had just had the sit-in in March at the courthouse with all those colored kids stirred up."

"Have you ever seen a colored boy or a colored man at her home or in the backyard of her house?"

"I saw some colored boys goin' in her front door one afternoon when I was walkin' home from work."

"More than one boy?"

"Three or four of them. I'm tryin' to think how many. There were some colored girls with them."

"A group then?"

"Yessir."

"Ever see just one colored boy or colored man comin' or goin'?"

"Not that I remember, but she had a lot of comins' and goins' since she taught piano lessons. I could hear the music in the afternoons—some good playin' and some pretty bad playin' on the piano."

"Now this man you saw on the mornin' after Easter—did he look at all familiar to you? Like maybe you had seen him before?"

"I didn't recognize his walk if that's what your askin', and he was all covered up. I wish I could've seen his face. His clothes were pretty baggy, and like I said he was wearin' a ball cap and gloves. He had his coat collar turned up in back. I just remembered that. I didn't see any skin."

"So he could have been colored or white. Would you agree?"

"Yessir. He could've been either one."

"You're not trying to say it was Jim Tressell you saw that morning, are you? You don't know for sure who that man was, do you?"

"No, sir, I don't know for sure who he was."

"No further questions, Your Honor."

Judge Harper looked at the jury then and said, "Gentlemen, I have to go out of town tomorrow to a conference in Texarkana. This was planned before this trial date was set. You'll have the day off from jury duty tomorrow, but you're not to speak a word about this trial to anyone—not your wife, not your neighbor, not your boss and not even your mother. Court will resume at 9:00 on Monday mornin'. You're dismissed for today and for the weekend."

When Mama and I had reached the bottom of the courthouse steps, Harry Price ran over to us.

"How'd I do up there on the stand? I told you I was gonna be a witness."

"You did just fine, Harry," said Mama. "You told the truth like you were supposed to."

"I did. Nothin' but the truth," he looked down at me. "Sorry I couldn't help your friend, Bobbi, but I couldn't say the man was colored when I didn't know for sure."

"I know," I told him. "I wish you'd seen him better that day. I don't think it was Mr. Tressell goin' in her yard."

"But you don't know that for sure," he said.

"Nobody knows for sure except the man who killed her," said Mama. "At least we have a break from the trial tomorrow and Saturday and Sunday. I know that Betsy and Mavis and Katie, too, will be happy to hear that. Let's head on home. You walkin' home now, Harry?"

"Yes, ma'am. I have the afternoon off work because of the trial."

"Walk with us, why don't you?"

"If you don't mind, I will."

Harry talked almost the whole way home about his customers and which shoes they liked best. When we reached the Tressells' house, he finally stopped talking about shoes and asked Mama how she thought Mrs. Tressell was doing.

"As good as can be expected, I guess," Mama said. "Under the circumstances."

"I thought that she couldn't walk at all," he said.

"She can't. They don't know what caused her illness. Jim took her to several doctors ten or so years ago. They couldn't help her. At least that's what he told Bobbi."

"Well, last week when I was walkin' home from work, I could almost swear I saw her standin' up and lookin' out her front window," Harry said.

"It must've been Jim Tressell's niece. She comes to check on her a couple of times a month, and it's not nice to swear, Harry."

"Sorry about that, but it sure looked like Mrs. Tressell. I've seen her in that window quite a few times before sittin' there in her wheelchair. She's always frownin'."

"I can't imagine her bein' able to walk. I usually go over there on Monday to get her grocery list, but I'll need to go tomorrow if we're goin' back to the courthouse on Monday. Maybe she's improvin'. I hope that's the case since she's been on her own since Jim was arrested," said Mama.

When we reached the Baxters' house, we told Harry good-bye and went up the side steps to get Betsy from Mavis. She invited us in for some lemonade. Mama told Mavis what was happening at the trial. Katie showed me all of the pictures she'd painted with her watercolors while I'd been going to the trial. I heard Mama ask Mavis if she had ever seen Mrs. Tressell walking inside her house or outside in the garden.

"Never have. I didn't think she could walk."

"Me either. Harry Price, the shoe salesman who testified today, said that he saw her standin' in her front window one afternoon. I think he must've been mistaken. You think I should ask her if she's gettin' better?"

"If it's not true, she'll just think you're meddlin' and get upset. If it's true, she might not want anybody to know," said Mavis. "Not wantin' to draw any more attention to herself right now, and she could've just been standin' up. Did he actually see her takin' any steps?"

Mama shook her head. "He just said he saw her standin'. "You're prob'ly right about upsettin' her, but if she can walk even a little, it seems she might wanna go to Jim's trial and show some support," said Mama.

"I doubt she's feelin' very supportive of him after the affair and bein' accused of murder."

"But it won't be good for her if he gets convicted, and it's sure lookin' like he will," whispered Mama.

"Maybe just ask her if she wants to go to the trial with you and Bobbi. See what she says. That shouldn't upset her. I don't mind watchin' Betsy at all next week. She's been as sweet as can be and has really kept Annie and Katie company, too."

"I can't tell you how much I appreciate your help. I'll have to make it up to you," Mama told her.

"Just keep fillin' me in on what's goin' on at the trial. That's enough for me."

"We best be goin' on home. I need to get supper started for Jack and the girls."

Mama gave Mavis a hug and picked Betsy up from the floor where she and Annie were playing. We headed home.

Before Daddy left to go to the field house on Saturday morning, Mama went to visit Mrs. Tressell who was in her wheelchair and acted the same way she had during all of Mama's other visits. Mama didn't say anything about Harry seeing someone standing in her front window or ask her about going with us to the trial. Mama told me she was pretty sure that Harry Price had been mistaken.

"Harry can be pretty dramatic, so I'm not sure we can go by what he says all the time."

"Was he bein' dramatic on the witness stand?" I asked Mama.

"He was just bein' Harry on the witness stand—a little silly and a little dramatic, too. I think he was tellin' the truth if that's what you're askin'."

"I think he was tellin' the truth, too. I wish the truth could've been different. He didn't have to tell the part about seein' them smoochin' in her garden. Nobody even asked him about that."

"I know. He just got carried away, but he wasn't able to say for sure that the man he saw was Jim. That was good for Jim's and Mr. Cornelius' side."

"But everybody still thinks he did it. I can just tell."

"I know it's not lookin' good for him."

On Monday morning we made our way into the courtroom again.

"Let's find our regular spots at the back," Mama said.

We said hello to the people around us as we sat down. Judge Harper came into the courtroom, we all stood, and the trial started up again.

"Mr. Craig, another witness?"

"Yes, Your Honor. The people call Mary Ross."

Mary Ross came in the back door of the courtroom. She was a lot older than Mama. She had gray hair that was pulled back into a bun, and she was wearing a floral dress that buttoned up the front. She looked a little like our next door neighbor, Mrs. Van Worth, with glasses on the end of her nose and a pinched-in face.

After she promised to tell the truth, she sat down and smoothed out her dress. Mr. Craig asked her to tell the jury about the day Mr. Tressell came into the flower shop to order roses. She explained that he ordered a dozen yellow roses on the morning of April 1st and had wanted to pay cash, but he didn't have enough money with him, so he wrote a check.

"Did he also give you the name and address of the person he was sendin' the roses to?"

"I asked him to write it down. It was the same person he bought roses for back in the fall around Thanksgiving. I remembered him because he was wearin' overalls both times and really didn't strike me as the kind of man who bought roses on a regular basis."

"Did he ask you to deliver the roses?"

"He did. We don't charge for deliverin'. I told him we were really busy with Easter deliveries, but we would do our best to get them to his lady friend either late that afternoon or early Monday mornin'."

"Did he have a problem with that?"

"He didn't seem to. I told him we could call him later that day to let him know about the delivery time for sure, but he told me not to call him. He was very clear about that. I said, 'All right.' Then he left the shop."

"Can you tell us when the roses were delivered?"

"No, sir. I'm sorry to say that I can't tell you for sure. We had a temporary delivery boy workin' for us that weekend. Just helpin' out with all of the Easter orders. It's one of our biggest weekends of the year. That order of roses was on his list of deliveries. The boy only worked for us that one weekend and the Monday after Easter. When the detective came around askin' questions about the roses, I told him the boy's name, but he couldn't locate him. He and his family had moved away from Marshall. The order could've been delivered on Saturday or on Monday. I just don't know which one."

"I have no further questions for Mrs. Ross, Judge," said Mr. Craig.

"Mr. Cornelius?"

"Just a couple, Your Honor." He stood at his table.

"What address did Jim Tressell write down on the note pad for you?"

"908 Rusk Street."

"Didn't you think it was a little odd that he lived on Rusk Street, too? You probably saw his address on his check."

"I really didn't notice."

"He lives at 809 Rusk. The number he wrote down for you was 908."

"Like I said, I didn't notice, but I do remember the name he wrote down. It was Lucille Harris, the lady who was murdered."

"No further questions, Your Honor."

The judge said, "You may step down, Mrs. Ross. "

"Mr. Craig?"

"The people rest, Your Honor," said Mr. Craig. I knew that meant he was finished calling witnesses. Now it would be Mr. Cornelius' turn.

Mr. Cornelius stood and told the judge that he was waiting on some important information to arrive and asked if he could call his first witness after lunch. The judge agreed and dismissed all of us until 2:00.

After the trial started up again at 2:00, Mr. Cornelius asked if he and Mr. Craig could come to the judge's bench. We couldn't hear what they were saying since they were all whispering. When they had finished talking, the lawyers went back to their tables.

"Mr. Cornelius has asked to call a witness who was not on the original list of witnesses. After hearing his reasons and conferring with Mr. Craig, I have agreed to allow the witness to testify," he explained to the jury.

"Mr. Cornelius, you may call your first witness," said the judge.

"The defense calls Richard D. Lambert, Your Honor."

A blonde-headed man with a big smile and white teeth walked through the door. He was wearing a brown suit, white shirt and green tie. He was what Daddy would call a square man. He was almost as wide as he was tall. Daddy liked square football players because they were strong and hard to tackle.

After Mr. Lambert promised to tell the truth, he sat down in the witness chair and let out a big puff of air.

"Mr. Lambert, are you out of breath?" asked Judge Harper.

"Just drove in from Texarkana and couldn't find a parkin' place. Had to circle the courthouse three times before someone pulled out. Didn't want to be late," he explained. He was a fast talker.

"Please state your name, date of birth, occupation and place of residence for the record."

"Richard D. Lambert. September 1, 1921. I'm a private investigator. I have my own business, Lambert Investigations, in Texarkana. Texarkana is split down the middle with part in Texas and part in Arkansas. I live on the Texas side of town."

After he promised to tell the truth, Mr. Cornelius asked him his first question.

"Can you tell the jury when you were first contacted about this trial?"

"Yessir. You called me on Thursday of last week and asked me to do some leg work for you."

"And what kind of leg work did I ask you to do?"

"You told me you had recently learned about a murder that was committed in Texarkana in March of 1950. You said that you wanted some information about the murder."

"Were you living in Texarkana at the time that murder was committed?"

"Yessir. I was a sergeant in the Texarkana Police Department from 1948 until 1955. That's when I left the department and got my private investigator's license."

"Was there any specific reason why you left the Texarkana PD?

"Just wanted to be home more with my family. Control my own hours. My best friends are still policemen."

"Were you part of the team that investigated the 1950 murder that I asked you to look into?"

"No, sir, but I knew the detective who was in charge, and I heard all about it during the investigation. You can't be part of a small town police force and not hear the details about a murder investigation."

"Is the detective who headed up the investigation part of the police force now?"

"He's retired, but he still lives in Texarkana. The murder case you called me about is the one that haunts him."

"Why is that, Mr. Lambert?"

"They never solved it. Had several suspects, but they all had ironclad alibis. There wasn't enough evidence either. No fingerprints at the scene, and no murder weapon was ever found."

"Can you tell us about this murder that took place in Texarkana in March of 1950?"

"I can tell you what was in the files at the department. I went by and had them pulled so that I could read through them after you called me. I also went by to visit Detective Gaines, the retired investigator I mentioned. I can tell you what he said, too, but I guess that would be hearsay, wouldn't it?"

"It would. Can you tell us what was in the department files?"

"A pretty young woman in her early twenties was attacked in her home early one mornin'."

"What time of day did this attack take place?"

"The estimated time was listed as that mornin'—not very specific, I know. The science has gotten a lot better in the last ten years."

"By morning do you mean 1:00 AM or 10:00 AM?"

"After 8:00 AM according to the police report. Someone was with her until 8:00 the mornin' of the attack."

"Would that have been her husband?"

He shook his head no. "She wasn't married. She was a single woman, but she was known to have had a number of entanglements if you know what I mean."

"Boyfriends?"

"Boyfriends who sometimes spent the night at her house."

"Was a boyfriend with her prior to 8:00 on the morning of the attack?"

"No, sir. Her mother had come in from Fort Worth to spend the weekend with her. She left her daughter's house right about 8:00 to drive back home. She was the last person to see her alive."

"So how was this young woman killed?"

"She was stabbed more than twenty times."

It seemed to me that everyone in the courtroom gasped at the same time.

"A crime of passion?"

"Passion, I don't know about. A crime of anger for sure."

"Can you tell us about the location of the stab wounds?"

"I studied the photos that were in the files. They were pretty awful to look at when I saw them back then and were still awful when I looked again this past Friday. She was stabbed all over her arms and then several times in her chest."

"Deep wounds in the chest?"

"Not really. Maybe 2 or 3 inches according to the documents, but they were near her heart. That's what killed her."

"Who discovered her body?"

"A co-worker came by to pick her up for work. They both worked down at the Piggly Wiggly as checkers. The victim didn't come outside when her friend honked her horn, so the friend went to her door. She called out her name, but nobody answered. The door was unlocked, so she went inside and found her lyin' on the floor of her livin' room."

"Face up or face down?"

"Face down in a lot of blood. I remember that the friend was really shaken up by it."

I started to shake then. I was afraid I might start crying, but Mama put her arm around my shoulders and hugged me to her.

"When the police arrived, did they find anything else unusual about the crime?"

"It was pretty obvious that she had been stabbed in the chest and then turned over after she was dead."

"Mr. Lambert, you've read the details that I gave you about the murder here in Marshall of Lucille Harris. Is that correct?"

"Yessir, I have."

"Do you see any similarities between the two murders?"

"Both women were young and attractive and lived alone. Both had stab wounds in the chest that killed them, and both were killed in their own homes in the mornin' hours."

"But that could be said of a lot of murders. Isn't that true?"

"That's true, all right, but the Texarkana murder and your murder here in Marshall have somethin' else in common."

"Can you tell us what that would be?"

Mr. Lambert looked around the courtroom. Everyone was waiting for his answer.

"When the Justice of the Peace arrived and pronounced Linda Lou Grubbs dead, the policemen who were on the scene turned her over and saw cuts that looked like Xs on both of her cheeks."

Everyone in the courtroom started talking then.

"Order," said the judge. "Order in this courtroom."

The talking continued, so Judge Harper called for a 30 minute recess.

⊷†⊶

Since we were sitting on the back row, we were some of the first people to leave the courtroom.

"We have time to get a Coke at Woolworth's if we don't dawdle. What do you say? Would you like that?" asked Mama.

"I sure would."

As she opened Woolworth's heavy glass door for me, I asked, "Is this the counter where the colored kids tried to order a sandwich?"

She nodded and said, "That was a sad day in Marshall."

The ceiling fans were spinning in Woolworth's. "It's cooler in here," I told her.

"Let's get those seats at the counter down there," she said and pointed to the far end of fifteen silver stools with red shiny material on the seats. Mama ordered two Cokes. The waitress smiled at me as she set the tall glasses with lots of ice on the counter in front of us.

"It's good and cold. Thanks for lettin' me have a Coke."

"You're very welcome," Mama said as she hugged me around the shoulders again. "I was hopin' this special little treat might make you feel better after what we heard this mornin' at the trial."

"It does." I took another big sip of my Coke.

"I can't believe that a woman in Texarkana got killed in the very same way as Lucille. It's just too terrible to even think about."

"Does it help Mr. Tressell or hurt him?"

"I'm sure that Mr. Cornelius thinks it'll help him. I don't know why else he'd want the jury to know about it."

Miss Lucille's brother walked up behind us then.

"Nita, Bobbi, afternoon," Larry Shaw said. We both turned around on our stools to face him.

"I didn't see you walk up, Larry," Mama said. She looked to her left and saw that all of the stools at the counter were taken. "Is Patty with you? Would you like our stools? We'll be finishin' up our Cokes in a few minutes."

"No, thanks. Patty needed to buy some bobby pins for her hair, so we walked over. We're headin' back over across the street. I guess all of what Mr. Lambert said came as a surprise to you, too."

"Shockin' really," said Mama.

I took another sip of my Coke.

"Can't believe that man could kill two women in such a gruesome way," he said.

"Do you think Jim killed the lady in Texarkana?"

"Sure sounds like it to me."

I turned around to look at Miss Lucille's brother.

"But Mr. Cornelius is supposed to help Mr. Tressell," I said to him.

"Doesn't make any sense to me either, but I think he must be a serial killer. I read about one called the Night Stalker in the Houston newspaper. He's killed at least five women, and he's still on the loose."

"Maybe he killed Miss Lucille," I said.

"His crimes have all been in California. I'm just saying that sometimes a serial killer can be living right here among us, and we don't even know it. Serial killers like to leave a sign like the X marks on the cheeks. Jim Tressell may have been killing women from 1950 until now."

"He wouldn't do that," I told him.

"I have a feeling we'll be hearing all about it," he said. "Better get back to Patty. She's checkin' out now." He turned to go. Mama paid for our Cokes, and we walked back to the courthouse and took our seats again.

Everyone was talking to their neighbors until Judge Harper came in. The courtroom got quiet.

"I expect all of you to abide by the rules of decorum the rest of the day. If you can't do that, I'll be forced to have you escorted outside. I want to be perfectly clear about that."

He looked at Mr. Cornelius who stood up and started his questioning again.

"Mr. Lambert, before the recess, you told us about the X marks on the cheeks of Linda Lou Grubbs. Had anyone in the Texarkana police department ever seen anything like that before?"

"No, sir. That was a first for all of us."

"So this wasn't a pattern?"

"Not until now," said Mr. Lambert.

"You mentioned that the Texarkana victim had a number of boyfriends. Did the report about the 1950 murder say if any of her boyfriends were suspects?"

"They were. Four boyfriends were brought in for questionin'."

"Did you know any of the four men?"

"I knew a couple of them. They were local. The other two lived outside of town. One of them lives here in Marshall now."

People started to look around at each other when he said that.

"And who would that be?"

"The defendant, Jim Tressell, was questioned about the murder in Texarkana."

Before any noise broke out again, Judge Harper hit his gavel on his desk.

"Why was my client questioned? Was he a suspect?"

"Like I said, Linda Lou Grubbs had had four boyfriends since movin' to Texarkana. He was one of the four."

"Did Jim Tressell have an alibi?"

"He did. He worked at the railroad then and was at work that mornin'."

"Worked a day shift then?"

"No, sir. The report said that he usually worked the night shift from 11 at night to 7 in the mornin', but he was doin' some mechanical work on a train over near Vivian, Louisiana that night and the followin' mornin'. They were havin' trouble with the brakin' system until after noon that next day, so the whole crew was late gettin' back to Texarkana. He said they got paid overtime."

"I want to be clear now. Are you saying that Jim Tressell was with a work crew in Vivian the morning that Linda Lou Grubbs was killed?"

"All four of the other crew members—the conductor, two brakemen and the engineer all swore on a stack of Bibles that he was with them the whole time. Jim Tressell's a fireman—the assistant to the engineer—so he was right there with his boss tryin' to get the brakes workin' that mornin'."

"So Jim Tressell could not have killed Linda Lou Grubbs?"

"No, sir. He didn't kill her."

"And what about the other boyfriends? You said they had alibis, too?"

"Yessir. According to his notes, Detective Gaines tried ever which way he could to break those men, but their alibis were tight. The investigation drug on, but without a witness or fingerprints or a murder weapon, it finally grew cold."

"Mr. Lambert, in your opinion, do you think that the person who killed Linda Lou Grubbs back in 1950 could be the same person who killed Lucille Harris?"

"I do. There are too many things that are the same in both cases."

"And Jim Tressell was cleared in the murder of Linda Lou Grubbs?"

"He couldn't have killed Miss Grubbs because he was workin' on a train over in Vivian, Louisiana the mornin' of the murder."

"Your witness, Mr. Craig."

Mr. Craig stood up and stayed behind his table.

"You can't be positive that the murder in Texarkana and the murder here in Marshall are connected, can you Mr. Lambert?"

"No, sir. I can't be positive, but…"

"Just answer the question, sir."

"Since the murder in Texarkana was never solved, there could be two different killers, couldn't there?"

"Yessir. There could be."

"Detective Gaines must've thought that the defendant over there at the table had a motive. Is that why he questioned him?"

"He questioned four men."

"What do you suppose the motive for the Texarkana murder could have been? Jealousy?"

"Objection," said Mr. Cornelius. "That calls for speculation."

"I'll withdraw the question, Your Honor," said Mr. Craig.

"For all any of us know, two different people could've committed these two murders? Isn't that correct?"

"Yessir," said Mr. Lambert.

"No further questions," said Mr. Craig, and he sat down.

Mr. Cornelius stood up again and asked if he could talk to the judge in chambers.

"We're almost to the end of our day anyway, so we'll adjourn now. Gentlemen, please meet me in ten minutes in my chambers. Court is dismissed until 9:00 o'clock tomorrow mornin'."

That afternoon Katie, Law and I were swingin' in the hammock next to Mrs. Tressell's house when we saw Detective Binotti drive up and park his car in front of Miss Lucille's empty house.

"C'mon, let's go." We ran up the street and sat down on the curb across from her house.

The detective walked around on her front porch for a few minutes. Then he went to the side yard and walked around some more. When he went to the backyard, we crossed the street and followed him.

"What's he doin'?" whispered Katie.

"He's lookin' for something," I said.

"I don't know what," added Law. "It's been a long time since the murder."

"Hey, Detective Binotti. Whatcha doin'?" I called out to him.

"Hey there," he said. "Just doin' some follow up. Are you still goin' to the trial, Bobbi? I saw you there with your mother."

"Yessir. I've been every day."

"We don't get to go," said Katie about herself and Law.

"Still playin' at your fort back there?" he asked.

"No, sir. We can't play there anymore," I said.

"Even though Mr. Tressell's in jail," added Law.

"You hear about the murder in Texarkana?" I asked him. "Sounds like a serial killer. I looked it up in the *World Book*. There are a lot of serial killers."

"Don't think this was a serial killer. You don't need to worry about that," he said.

"Did you ever catch the Peepin' Tom?" asked Law.

"Not yet."

"It's been a long time ago," I told him. "He was wearin' a ball cap like the man who came into Miss Lucille's backyard that day."

"I remember that," said the detective.

"You gonna warn Miss Lottie that the Peepin' Tom could've been a serial killer?"

"I don't plan to. Mr. Tressell's in jail."

"But he didn't kill the lady in Texarkana. He had an alibi. They said it in court."

"It could have been a copycat murder," he said.

"I heard about that on Perry Mason. It's someone who hears about a murder and then copies the way it was done," Law said.

"That's right."

"You think Mr. Tressell copied the murder in Texarkana. Even the X marks on the cheeks?" I asked.

"I hate it that you kids have to hear about all these things. It's safe here where you live. All this is makin' you grow up too fast. Is your mother home, Bobbi?"

"Yessir. Prob'ly ironin'."

"Don't wanna be a bother, but I'd like to ask her a question."

"I can check."

"That would be good."

I ran toward my house.

Katie and Law were talking to the detective when I got back.

"She said for you to come on over."

"Thanks." He walked toward our house, and we followed him.

"You can go in the back door. Mama's in the den with Betsy."

Mama saw us coming and opened the screen door for him.

"Can we play *Authors*, Mama?"

"If you'll watch Betsy while I talk to Detective Binotti." She handed my little sister to me.

Katie got the card game out of the kitchen drawer. We sat down on the den floor. Mama and Detective Binotti sat at the kitchen table.

"You can deal," Katie told Law.

As we started our game, I heard the detective tell Mama that he was just tying up some loose ends. He wanted to be sure about everything in his investigation since a man might be going to the electric chair.

"How long have you known the Tressells?" he asked Mama.

"Almost eight years, I think. Bobbi was a little older than Betsy when we moved to Rusk Street. The Tressells were already livin' here. They moved here a couple of years before we did. Mavis and Howard Baxter, across the street, were livin' here when they moved in. Mavis might know more, but the Tressells are hard to get to know. She's always kept to herself. I think she must be in pain some with her legs. Either that or she's just not a people person."

"What about him?"

"He came to our July the 4th picnics every year, but he's really quiet. You know Jack is a talker, and even he couldn't get him to say much. He met Lucille at our picnic."

"Not long after she moved to Rusk Street?"

"She moved here at the first of the summer, so about a month after that."

"Did his wife come to the picnics?"

"She never came. He always brought fresh tomatoes from his garden. I think that's why he came, to share his tomatoes. Everybody loved them and told him so. He was so proud of that garden of his."

"He ever mention his time in Texarkana?"

"At the trial is the first time I even knew they'd lived there."

"I heard you've been goin' to check on her, helpin' her with her groceries. That's mighty neighborly of you."

"Just tryin' to help out. Seems like the right thing to do. She's all by herself and can't walk."

"I wanted to ask you about that—her illness."

"I don't really know much."

"I've heard from a couple of people that maybe she's gettin' better. Able to walk a little bit now."

"She hasn't said anything to me. Always in her wheelchair when I go over there. Harry Price told me one day that he saw her standin' in her front window, but you know Harry. I told him it must've been Jim's niece."

"The older Mr. Baxter stopped by my office last week. He said that he'd seen someone walkin' about in the Tressells' garden. He was worried for her safety and for his family's safety what with his chicken house bein' the place the knife was found."

Katie, Law and I looked at each other.

"Who could it be? Should we keep the kids inside?"

"Don't think you need to worry. He said it looked like a woman—long hair hangin' down her back."

"Maybe Jim's niece."

"How often does she come to visit?"

"A couple of times a month—on Saturday. That's what Ruth told me."

Katie sat her cards down, stood up and walked over to the kitchen table.

"I saw Mrs. Tressell through the window this mornin' standin' in front of her TV," she told them. "Law was with me. We were swingin' in the hammock."

"And you could see inside her house?" Detective Binotti asked her.

Katie nodded. "When the hammock is goin' high, you can. Law was swingin' me, and I saw her. Standin' there by the TV and then walkin' around."

"Maybe she's gettin' better. Maybe she's had to make herself better since Jim's not around to help," said Mama.

Katie sat back down and picked up her cards.

"Possible," he said. "When are you goin' back over there again?"

"Not until Saturday since we're goin' to the trial every day. Do I need to go sooner than that?"

"I was thinkin' I might get you to go over there with me."

"Today?"

"Maybe tomorrow. I should call her first."

"Tomorrow's better for me. I need to start supper now. We'll be home from the trial by 4:30. It's been endin' around 4:00. That'll give us time to walk home and pick up Betsy."

"I'll come by tomorrow about 4:30 and park out front. We'll walk over together. That is if she'll be home," he said.

"I'm sure she will be. She hasn't been comin' to the trial, and she doesn't drive."

185

"I'll let myself out then," he said as he stood up from the table.

"Bye, Detective Binotti," I called out.

He waved his white hat at us and then put it on his head as he went out the back door of our den.

———⊰ ⊱———

The next day at the trial, Mr. Cornelius called four different men who worked with Mr. Tressell at the railroad to come to the stand.

The first man was older and looked even stronger than Mr. Tressell. His name was Walter Freeman, and he said he was an engineer at the T & P Railroad.

"Good morning, Mr. Freeman. Thank you for coming to the courthouse today. I'm guessing you worked the night shift last night. Is that correct?"

"Yessir. I did."

"I know this is an inconvenience, but hopefully, you can get some sleep after your testimony. Can you tell us how you know the defendant, Jim Tressell?"

"He's my fireman at T & P—my assistant. He works for me."

"Would you say that he's a hard worker?"

"Yessir. He's a very hard worker."

"How long has he worked with you at T & P?"

"Around ten years. I don't have his start date in my head, but he's been there a long time now. Transferred here from Texarkana."

"Did he ever say much to you about when he worked in Texarkana?"

"No, sir, just that Marshall had a bigger yard and was a better opportunity for him."

"Nothing about any problems when he lived in Texarkana?"

"No, sir. I wouldn't know anythin' about any problems. Always did good work for me."

"Would you say then that he's dependable?"

"Yessir."

"Miss work much?"

"Never that I can remember. He carried his load."

"Did he ever talk about his wife?"

"Just when he first started work here. Said that he had taken her to some doctors over in Shreveport. That somethin' was wrong with her legs. She couldn't walk. I didn't ask any questions. Don't like to pry in personal matters."

"Did he ever mention any other women?"

"No, sir. Jim's not much of a talker. When he did talk, he talked about his garden. He liked to share his vegetables with us at the yard. He can grow just about anything." He looked over at Mr. Tressell.

"Were you surprised when he was arrested?"

"Yessir. It's still hard for me to believe it."

"Ever see him get in any fights with other men at the yard?"

"Never. He's quiet. Good, hard worker."

"Doesn't have a bad temper?"

"Not that I've ever seen."

"No further questions, Your Honor."

Mr. Craig stood up and walked over to the witness stand.

"Mr. Freeman, did you ever spend time with Jim Tressell outside of work?"

"No, sir. Just at the railroad."

"So you don't know what kind of man he is away from work. Do you?"

"I don't think he would be much different."

"But you don't know for sure if he has a drinkin' problem, a runnin' around problem, a bad temper at home. Do you?"

"I think I could've have spotted somethin' like that workin' together for ten years."

"Please answer the question, sir. Can you know for sure what somebody's like away from his job if you never spent any time with him outside of work?"

"No, sir. I can't know for sure."

"So he could have a temper, he could beat his wife, he could even have a motive to stab somebody, but you couldn't know that, could you?"

"Objection," said Mr. Cornelius. "He's badgering the witness."

"Sustained," said the judge. "Is that all, Mr. Craig?"

"Yes, Your Honor."

"Mr. Freeman, you may step down. Go on home and get some sleep," Judge Harper told him.

The next three witnesses were also from the railroad. One was a conductor, and two were brakemen. They made up the rest of Mr. Tressell's crew at T & P.

Mr. Cornelius asked them the same questions he had asked Mr. Freeman. Like him, all of them said that Mr. Tressell was a hard worker and was dependable and had never had any problems at work.

Mr. Craig asked them all if they knew Mr. Tressell outside of work, and they didn't. He asked them if they knew about any problems in Texarkana and if Mr. Tressell had a temper. They all told him no.

At the end of the day, Mama and I decided that this was the first day that anyone had said good things about Mr. Tressell at the trial. The men he worked with all liked him and thought he was a hard worker. Mr. Craig tried to get them to say bad things about him, but they wouldn't do it.

That afternoon Detective Binotti came to our house at 4:30. The four of us walked over to Mrs. Tressell's house. She came to the front door in her wheelchair and let us come inside. Mama asked me to watch Betsy in Mrs. Tressell's small living room while she and Detective Binotti went into her TV room. It was close enough that I could hear them talking.

"We wanted to stop by to see how you're doin'," he told her. "To see if you need medicine or a doctor or anything."

"About time somebody asked. You arrested my husband and left me here to fend for myself in this chair." She sounded mad.

"Hasn't Jim's niece been helpin' with your medicine, Ruth?" Mama asked.

"She has."

"I don't think I've ever met her. Is this a picture of her with Jim?" Mama said. "She's a pretty girl with all that long brown hair."

"She's the only one of his family who cares."

"I wanted to ask you about when you lived in Texarkana," said Detective Binotti.

"What about it?"

"How long did you live there?"

"Five years—moved there after I married 'im."

"When was that?"

"Summer of 1945. We lived on a farm where he grew up. Then he got on at the railroad."

"Did you like livin' on a farm?"

"I liked it better than havin' him work the night shift, but the railroad paid better. Had benefits."

"You moved to Marshall—about 1950?"

"1951."

"What brought you to Marshall?" Mama asked her.

"My illness started up. He took me to some doctors over in Shreveport. Ran all kinds of tests on me, but nobody could tell us nothin'. Been in this chair ever since. He sold the farm in Texarkana, and we bought this place when T & P had an openin' for a fireman. That's his job. It was a raise in pay. Bigger yard here. One of the biggest in the southwest."

"Has the railroad been supportin' you?"

"While he's been in jail?"

"Yes."

"They have."

"Who's helpin' you with the garden?" asked Detective Binotti.

"Nobody."

"A neighbor saw somebody in your garden last week."

"Somebody tryin' to take advantage and steal my vegetables while he's in jail?"

"I don't think so. Your neighbor was concerned for your safety. You might wanna lock your doors."

"You remember we had a Peepin' Tom last summer don't you, Ruth?"

"I can take care of myself."

"Have you remembered anything else about the day Mrs. Harris was killed that might help your husband?"

"Why do you care? You're the one who arrested him."

"Just doin' my job, ma'am."

"I didn't know anythin' then, and I don't know anythin' now. I was asleep on the couch. He ever talk about it?"

"Only to say he didn't do it," he told her.

"These questions are wearin' me out. Time to take my medicine and get my supper goin'."

"Sorry to have bothered you. If you don't mind, I'd like to take another look around the garden."

"Suit yourself."

"I'll be by on Saturday to get your grocery list," Mama told her. "C'mon girls, we better be goin'. I've got supper to fix, too."

When we were on the porch, Detective Binotti thanked Mama for coming with him.

"I hope it helped. She looks the same to me, and she's pretty bitter," Mama said. "I did notice in the picture that Jim's niece has long hair. Maybe she was the lady Tada saw in their garden."

"Could be," he said. Then he nodded and headed toward Mr. Tressell's garden.

⊨⊰ ⊱⊨

We didn't go to court the next morning because the judge had some hearings on other cases. Mr. Tressell's trial started again after lunch at 1:30.

After Judge Harper and the jury were seated, we all sat down.

"Call your first witness, Mr. Cornelius," said the judge.

"The defense calls Ruth Tressell."

"She didn't say anything to us yesterday about bein' a witness," Mama whispered to me. "I'm surprised she's here."

The guard at the back of the courtroom opened the door, and I saw a policeman pushing Mrs. Tressell in her wheelchair down the aisle toward the witness stand. Her long brown hair was pulled back in a ponytail like mine. She was wearing a pink cotton dress with a white collar and no lipstick. She was sitting low in her wheel chair and leaning forward. Daddy would say that she needed to sit up straight and hold her shoulders back.

"Since we don't have an easy way to get your wheelchair onto the witness stand, I'm goin' to have you sworn in and let you give your testimony right down there in front."

Mrs. Tressell shared her name, her birthdate of October 4, 1922, that she was a housewife and a Marshall resident. She put her hand on the Bible and promised to tell the truth.

"Is the defendant, Jim Tressell, your husband?" Mr. Cornelius asked her.

"Yes."

"You understand that because of spousal privilege, you did not have to testify today. Is that correct?"

"Yes."

"You waived that privilege?"

"I did. You said you needed me to be here. You also said that if I didn't come, you would subpoena me. I came even though it's hard for me." She looked at Mr. Tressell. He was looking down at the table.

"How long have you and the defendant been married?"

"Sixteen years."

"And you lived in Texarkana after you first married?"

"Yes."

"When did you move to Marshall?"

"1951."

"Ten years ago?"

"Yes."

"Why did you leave Texarkana?"

"He got a better job with the railroad, and I was sick."

"How did your being sick necessitate a move to Marshall?"

"My doctors were in Shreveport. It was closer to them, but mainly it was the job that brought us here. The doctors couldn't help me."

"Can you tell us what type of illness you have?"

"I don't know a name for it if that's what you mean. I can't walk. My leg muscles don't work, and they hurt."

"Your legs hurt?"

"Yes. All the time. They're hurtin' right now."

"I'll move along with my questions. You said that your husband works for the railroad here in Marshall?"

"He did until he got arrested."

"The night shift?"

"Yes."

"What were his hours?"

"Eleven to seven, but he never got home before about 8:30 or 9:00. He liked to work overtime when he could. At least that's what he told me."

"When he got home from work, were you usually awake?"

"I usually heard him come in. The night shift is hard. You have to sleep durin' the day if you work at night."

"Did you normally sleep during the day when he slept?"

"I tried to, but sometimes I was tired and went to sleep before he got home."

"What time did he get home on the morning that Lucille Harris was killed?"

"I don't know. I was asleep on the couch in the living room. My legs hurt bad, so I took one of my pain pills and got myself onto the couch and went sound asleep."

"So your husband could've come home at 7:30 that morning?"

"I didn't hear him come in."

"Did he usually go right to bed when he got home, or did he eat breakfast first?"

"Sometimes he ate breakfast first. Sometimes he worked in the garden first before it got too hot. Sometimes he showered off before he went to sleep."

"Did you hear the water in the bathroom running on the morning Lucille Harris was killed?"

"I told you I was sound asleep on the couch. I didn't hear nothin' 'til I woke up at 11:30."

"Where was your husband when you woke up at 11:30?"

"In the bed asleep."

"Did you see anything unusual in the bedroom?"

"Like what?"

"Dirty clothes on the floor maybe?"

"Or bloody clothes, if that's what you're askin'?"

"Or bloody clothes?"

"Nothin' was on the floor. His work overalls were in the wash room in the basket."

"Do you own any Cutco knives?"

"Two or at least we did. We have one now."

"When did you notice the second one was missin'?"

"After the police came to our house and wanted to see 'em. My husband told me he could only find one."

"So the second knife could have been missing for a good while?"

"We used those knives most every day."

"But could it have been missing before Lucille Harris was murdered? Could someone have stolen it?"

"You mean come into our house with me in there and gotten one of our knives?"

"Isn't that possible?"

"Not hardly."

"In thinking about your relationship with your husband, would you say that he's a good provider?"

"He works hard."

"Does he drink to excess?"

"He doesn't drink. His daddy was an alcoholic, so he stays away from it."

"Has he ever hit you?"

"No."

"Has he ever slapped you?"

"No."

"Has he ever called you names?"

"No."

"Has he been supportive of you since your illness started?"

"Yes."

"Would you say then that he's a good husband?"

Mrs. Tressell looked at Mr. Tressell. Then she looked at Mr. Cornelius.

"No. He's not a good husband."

Mr. Cornelius looked surprised by her answer.

"Judge, I would like to request that you declare Ruth Tressell a hostile witness."

"Request is granted."

"He's a good provider. He's never hit you or slapped you. He doesn't drink, and he supports you by taking you to your doctors. But he's not a good husband?"

She looked mad when she said, "He couldn't keep his hands off those women."

The courtroom was very quiet.

"Which women are you talking about, Mrs. Tressell?"

"The one in Texarkana and the one that lived on the corner of our street."

"The two women who were murdered?"

"Yes."

"Did you know either of the women?"

"Both."

"Can you tell us how you knew them?"

"One of 'em worked at the Piggly Wiggly where I shopped. Wore too much makeup and that tight uniform showin' off her chest. Always flirtin' with them men."

"And Mrs. Harris?"

"Came to our house once to see his garden. Wearin' hardly anythin'. Both of 'em were sluts if you ask me."

Judge Harper said, "Please watch your language, ma'am."

She turned her head and squinted her eyes up at him.

Before Mr. Cornelius could ask his next question, I heard the back door to the courtroom open. A policeman led Harry Price, Katie and Tada down to the front row where they sat down behind Mr. Tressell's table. I looked at Mama. She shrugged her shoulders. We hadn't heard that they were coming to the trial.

Mr. Cornelius waited until they sat down and then turned back to look at Mrs. Tressell. She was looking at Harry, Tada and Katie.

"I believe you said that you haven't been able to walk since 1951? Is that correct?"

"Right before we moved here to Marshall is when I got sick."

"And your doctors never told you the name of your illness? Isn't that a little odd that they wouldn't know what to call it?"

"You'd have to ask them. They didn't tell me."

"And you haven't been able to walk at all since that time?"

"I haven't."

"What if I told you that three people have seen you walking recently?"

"They'd be lyin'."

"All three of them?"

"I said they're liars." Her voice was louder now.

"One of them saw you in your front window, one saw you in your garden and the third one saw you through your kitchen window."

"They made it up. I can't walk."

"Mrs. Tressell, you're under oath. If you lie, you're in danger of perjuring yourself. That means jail time and a big fine. Please answer the question. Can you walk?"

She didn't answer at first, and then she said, "Maybe I can walk a little. I seem to be gettin' better lately."

"So the three people who saw you walking and are in the courtroom today are not liars after all."

She stared at Harry, Katie and Tada.

"I said I can walk a little. I have to becuz he's in jail," she said and pointed at Mr. Tressell.

"Ah, yes, the man you said is not a good husband."

"He's not. He had affairs with those women."

"Linda Lou Grubbs and Lucille Harris?"

"Yeh. Them."

"How did you know about the affairs?"

"Wife just knows."

"Did you follow him to see where he was going when he went to their houses?"

"No."

"Are you sure about that? You're under oath."

She didn't answer.

"Did you hate him for breaking his marriage vow to you?"

"They ruined my marriage!"

"You hated those women, didn't you? You wanted to punish him, didn't you? You hated him for choosing those pretty women over you, didn't you?"

"They weren't pretty!"

"You moved to Marshall to get away from Texarkana after his first affair, didn't you?"

"No!"

"You made up your illness to punish him after what happened in Texarkana, didn't you?"

"No!"

"You had to stop him, didn't you?"

"I hope he rots in hell for sleepin' with those sluts and however many others there were."

Some people in the courtroom gasped.

"You hope he rots in hell for having affairs, but not for killing those women? Your husband didn't murder those women, did he? Because you know who murdered those women."

"Mr. Cornelius is yellin' at her, Mama," I whispered.

"Shhh, Bobbi." She patted my hand. "He knows what he's doin'."

"Had he ever sent you roses?"

"No."

"You were surprised when the yellow roses arrived at your house the day before Easter, weren't you?"

Mrs. Tressell just stared at him.

"The delivery boy made a mistake. He got the house numbers mixed up and delivered the roses to 809—your home instead of 908—Lucille Harris' house. When you saw the card, what did you think?"

"You're wrong!"

"You were angry, weren't you? You knew then he was having another affair. Did you hide the roses until Monday morning?'

"No!"

"Did you make your plan on Easter Sunday to go to her house on Monday morning and kill her?"

"No!"

"Did you put on his clothes, his gloves, his shoes and tuck your hair into one of his ball caps?"

"I did not!"

"You hid the roses inside your coat and put one of your sharp Cutco knives in your pocket. You were ready, weren't you? After all, you'd done this once before in Texarkana, hadn't you?"

"You're lyin'!"

"You came in from the side street hoping no one would notice and went to her back door. Did she think you were a delivery man? Did you smile when you handed her the roses?"

"Shut up!"

"You had to stop his affair, so you stabbed her over and over until she died. Then you cut her pretty face, turned her over and pushed her face into the floor, didn't you? You know who killed Lucille Harris because you did it!"

"I hate you!"

"You'd like to stab me right now, wouldn't you?"

Mrs. Tressell put her head back and screamed. Judge Harper hit his gavel on his desk.

"Order in the court," he said. "Mrs. Tressell, please try to compose yourself."

She put her head in her hands. She was crying.

Mr. Cornelius said, "No further questions, Your Honor. The defense rests."

"Mr. Craig?" the judge asked.

"No questions for this witness, Your Honor."

"Guard, please escort the witness from the courtroom," said Judge Harper. Everyone watched as the policeman pushed Mrs. Tressell in her wheelchair down the aisle and out the back door. She was still crying.

"Gentlemen, we'll hear your closing arguments tomorrow mornin' at 9:00 o'clock. Members of the jury, you're dismissed for today, and court is adjourned."

We waited until the judge, the jury and Mr. Tressell had left the courtroom. Then everyone started talking. Mama and I made our way to the front where Mr. Cornelius was talking to Harry, Katie and Tada.

Katie ran over to me and said, "The trial is so excitin'! I was so scared when she screamed!"

"Me, too," I told her. "Nothin' like that happened on any of the other days."

"I told you she could walk, didn't I?" Harry asked Mama.

"You were right, Harry."

"What happens now?" Tada asked Mr. Cornelius.

"We give our closing arguments tomorrow morning, the judge will give his instructions and then it's in the jury's hands."

"Surely they won't find Jim guilty now, not after this," said Mama.

"I hope not, but you never know until the jury comes back in," explained Mr. Cornelius. "I need to talk to my client now." To Tada, Katie and Harry, he said, "Thanks again for coming today." He picked up his papers from the desk, put them in his briefcase and left the courtroom.

"I didn't know you were comin'," I said to Katie.

"Me either until last night. Mr. Cornelius called Tada and asked if we could come. He said all we had to do was come in when the policeman told us to and sit on the front row."

"Mr. Cornelius called me, too. I thought at first that he wanted me to testify again, but he just wanted me to sit there and look at her and let her look at me. I knew she could walk. We all saw her, and she saw us, too. I didn't know a woman could be so mean," said Harry.

"Of the devil if you ask me," said Tada.

"I knew Mr. Tressell didn't do it," I said.

"I hope the jury agrees with you," Mama said. "We better be goin' now. We have a lot to tell your daddy, don't we?"

"Will this be the last day of the trial for sure?" I asked Mama after we took our seats in the courtroom. Mavis had let Katie come with us today.

"I think so after what Mr. Cornelius told us yesterday. It'll be the jury's time startin' today."

Judge Harper and the men on the jury came in. We all stood and then sat back down.

"What happens next?" asked Katie.

"The judge'll tell us."

"Mr. Craig, are you ready with your closing argument?" he asked the district attorney.

"I am, Your Honor."

"Proceed."

"Mornin' gentlemen. At the beginnin' of this trial, I told you that it was my responsibility to bring the case of the People versus Jim Tressell before you. He has been accused of murdering Lucille Harris by stabbin' her twenty-two times until she died.

"We've told you that he was havin' an adulterous affair with the victim—that he violated the 8th commandment of our Lord. When Mrs. Harris wanted to put a stop to this sordid affair, he murdered her in a fit of rage or of passion. Either way she ended up dead on her kitchen floor. At the beginnin' of this trial, you saw for yourself the gruesome photos.

"We showed you the murder weapon which was found in a chicken house near the defendant's home. His fingerprints were found on that murder weapon and in almost every room of the victim's home.

"But most significant of all, the defendant does not have an alibi for the time of the murder. He says he was asleep, but no one can confirm his claim.

"You heard a witness say he saw a man goin' into the victim's backyard on the mornin' she was murdered. We submit to you that man was the defendant. He went to her back door and went inside. They had an argument, and he got mad and killed her. It's as simple as that.

"The defense has tried to confuse you with a lot of gibberish about a murder in Texarkana that has nothin' to do with the murder here in Marshall and with a wife who can supposedly walk even though she has been confined to a wheelchair for ten years.

"I ask you not to let all of this crazy talk take your eyes off the ball. The defendant, Jim Tressell, killed Lucille Harris in her home on the morning of April 3th. I ask you to come back to this court with a verdict of guilty."

Mr. Craig walked back to his table and sat down.

"Mr. Cornelius, you may proceed with your closing statement," said Judge Harper.

"Thank you, Judge Harper. Gentlemen, thank you for doing your civic duty by serving on this jury. I know this hasn't been an easy task, but I also know you realize that a man's life is in your hands.

"Mr. Craig has told you that the defendant, Jim Tressell, is the person who killed Lucille Harris. I would guess that at the beginning of this trial, most of you would've thought that to be true, but I ask you to look at the facts that we've learned during this past week and a half.

"Fact number 1: The prosecutor hasn't brought forth anyone who can definitively place Jim Tressell at the scene of the crime on the morning of April 3rd. The closest person he had to a witness, Mr. Price, couldn't even tell you the height of the person he saw going into Mrs. Harris' backyard that day. We heard his testimony that this person was covered from head to toe, so this person could've been a woman or a man, colored or white. Mr. Price couldn't say.

"Fact number 2: The knife that was used to kill Mrs. Harris could've easily been stolen from Jim Tressell's kitchen. Like many of the citizens of Marshall, Jim Tressell trusted people. He didn't lock his doors, so anyone could've come into his house and taken that Cutco knife from his kitchen drawer. We submit that Jim Tressell's fingerprints were on the knife because that knife belonged to him. He'd been using that knife to chop vegetables from his garden before someone else took it and used it to stab Mrs. Harris. No other fingerprints were identified because the prosecutor didn't ask for any other fingerprints to be identified.

"Fact number 3: Any number of people could've gone into Mrs. Harris' home on the morning of April 3rd—colored boys she taught at Bishop College or the Peepin' Tom who had looked in a neighbor's window and was never caught or someone who was just passing by her house, noticed a pretty lady and then followed her inside. We have proven reasonable doubt in this case.

"Fact number 4: You've heard testimony that a similar murder was committed in Texarkana in 1950. This is not crazy talk as Mr. Craig has called it. I know that Linda Lou Grubbs' family wouldn't call it that. Miss Grubbs was stabbed the same number of times as Lucille Harris—twenty-two, and the same calling card was left on both of the victims—X marks on their cheeks. It sure sounds like the same person murdered both of them. You heard testimony from private investigator Lambert that Jim Tressell couldn't have killed Linda Lou Grubbs in Texarkana. He was nowhere near Texarkana that morning. He was in Vivian, Louisiana with a crew of four other men working on a train on the morning Linda Lou was killed.

"Fact number 5: You heard Jim Tressell's wife accuse him of having affairs with the victim in Texarkana and with Lucille Harris. My client would be the first to tell you that he made some mistakes. He broke his marriage vows, and he regrets those actions, but he's not on trial here for adultery. He's on trial for killing a woman. You cannot in good conscience find him guilty because Jim Tressell's not a murderer.

"Fact number 6: I think we know who had the most to gain from the murder of Lucille Harris. We know who had the passion and hate in her heart to stab Lucille Harris twenty-two times and to disfigure her face with X marks. We know who was sick and tired of her husband's affairs—so sick and tired of it that she made a plan to do something about it. Ruth Tressell had the motive, the opportunity and the means to kill Lucille Harris in a way that would not only punish Mrs. Harris but would point the finger of guilt at her husband. She wore his clothes, she used their knife that had his fingerprints on it, and she hid that knife in their neighbor's chicken house where it would be found. She pretended that she was crippled, but you heard her admit on the stand that she can walk. She chose that wheelchair to cover up two murders.

"I think we'd all agree this is a very sad case. A young woman has been murdered, and a marriage has been destroyed. However, don't let your emotions get the best of you. Jim Tressell made mistakes, but he didn't kill Lucille Harris. Ruth Tressell killed Lucille Harris and wanted our legal system to kill her husband Jim.

"I ask you to let this good man get on with his life. Come back to this court with a verdict of not guilty."

Mr. Cornelius turned and walked back to the table and sat down next to Mr. Tressell.

Judge Harper looked at the men on the jury and told them what they were supposed to do next. He said it was their duty to find out what was true. Then he told them they could leave to go to their jury room. He stood up and left, and the trial was over.

⊷⊶

Two days later, we heard the good news from Harry Price who called us on the telephone from the Hub Shoe Store. The jury decided Mr. Tressell was not guilty. I hugged Mama when she told me.

"Will he get to come home now?" I asked her.

"I'm sure he will," she said. "Harry also told me that Detective Binotti arrested Ruth. She'll be put on trial for killin' Lucille."

"I've gotta go tell Katie and Law!"

Mama was already dialing Daddy's telephone number at the field house. She waved to me as I went out the back door.

"Kee-Wo-Kee-K-A-T, Kee-Wo-Kee-K-A-T!" I called out at the bottom of Katie's stairs. I heard her door open, and she bounded down the steps. "Not guilty! Mr. Tressell's not guilty! I knew he didn't do it."

Katie jumped up and down and said, "Let's go tell Law."

We ran to Law's back door and knocked. Mrs. Lawrence came to the door.

"We have somethin' real important to tell Law," I told her.

"He's cleanin' Alvin's cage in the kitchen. Go on in there."

We hurried past her. She followed behind us.

"Law, he's not guilty. Mr. Tressell didn't do it!" I told him.

"That's good," he said. "Who did it?"

"They arrested Mrs. Tressell. She hated Miss Lucille."

"Well, don't that beat all," said Mrs. Lawrence. "I never would've thought she could kill someone bein' in a wheelchair."

"She can walk. I saw her. So did Tada and Harry Price," Katie told her.

"I heard about all that, but I still don't know if I believe it."

"Mama said she believes it."

"Tada said Mrs. Tressell's of the devil," said Katie.

"It seems like we had a lot of the devil's work goin' on here on Rusk Street," added Mrs. Lawrence as she left the kitchen.

"Wanna come outside with us, Law?"

"As soon as I finish cleanin' this cage."

"Meet us at the hammock."

"How 'bout the fort?" he asked.

The following week Detective Binotti called and asked Mama if he could come by to visit with our family. They decided on a time when Daddy would be home, too.

"Thanks for makin' time to see me," he told us. We all sat down in our den, and Mama brought him some coffee.

"How is Ruth doin'? Is she still in jail?" Mama asked.

"She'll be there until her trial just like her husband was."

"Has anybody checked on Jim since the trial ended?"

"Mr. Cornelius may have. I don't think he'd be interested in havin' me drop by."

"Maybe I could make him a pie. The girls and I could take it over unless you can go with us, Jack. Just check to see how he's doin'."

"Well find a time when I can go, too," said Daddy as he patted her hand.

Detective Binotti cleared his throat and said, "Your family was such a help to our department, and you were at the trial every day. I thought it was only right to give you some of the details about the case that have come to light, but it's off the record."

"All right," said Mama.

"You know the private investigator who testified at the trial?"

"Mr. Lambert from Texarkana?"

"Yes, ma'am. After Jim Tressell heard about the X marks on Lucille Harris' face, he told Rufus Cornelius about the Texarkana murder."

"That was the first time Mr. Tressell talked to Mr. Cornelius during the trial. I saw him lean over and whisper something to him," I told them before Detective Binotti continued.

"I think Jim knew then that his wife was involved. Rufus asked Mr. Lambert to do some follow up work with the detective who had investigated Linda Lou Grubbs' murder back in '50. The detective told Mr. Lambert he never could prove it, but he was pretty sure that Ruth Tressell had killed Linda Lou. Her other boyfriends had alibis and weren't married at the time, so Ruth was the only one with a motive. It was pretty common knowledge that she didn't care for Linda Lou. Also, when Judge Harper attended that conference in Texarkana during Jim Tressell's trial—you remember he had to be out for a day—a fellow judge suggested someone needed to take a good look at the wife. They couldn't pin it on her in Texarkana, but with the way the victims were attacked and cut, he thought it must be the same killer."

"Ever arrest anybody in that case?"

"No, Coach. It's never been solved."

"Until now, maybe."

Detective Binotti continued, "After the trial ended I took it upon myself to track down the delivery boy who worked at Rainbow Floral over Easter weekend when Lucille Harris was killed. It took some doin', but I finally found him and his family livin' over in Haughton, Louisiana. He's just a kid—seventeen. I wanted to know if he delivered the yellow roses to the wrong house like Mr. Cornelius said at the trial. The boy told me he remembered deliverin' yellow roses to a lady who was in a wheelchair. He asked her if he could take them inside for her since they were in a glass vase, and she told him no. She took the roses and closed the door.

It sounded like Mrs. Tressell to me.

"Those were the only yellow roses he delivered. All of the others were red," said Detective Binotti. "I knew then that Ruth Tressell got the roses. She probably read the card and realized they weren't for her. That told her that Jim and Lucille were more than good friends.

"My guess is when Jim went to see Lucille on Easter—you saw him arrive, Bobbi—he thought that since she hadn't gotten the roses, they'd be delivered on Monday. Remember Mary Ross at Rainbow Floral told him it could be either Saturday or Monday since they were so busy makin' deliveries. And he didn't want her to call his house to tell him which day for sure.

"Gettin' back to Ruth. I think she hid the roses from him and made her plans. When Jim got home from work on Monday mornin', she pretended to be asleep on the couch. This was most likely a common occurrence, so he wouldn't have bothered her. He changed his clothes and went to sleep.

"When she was sure he was sound asleep, she put on some of his clothes, his cap, his work boots and his gloves. She tucked her hair up inside the cap and put one of their Cutco knives in her pocket. She hid the flowers inside the coat that was too big for her and set out on her walk to Lucille's house. She went the back way—Morrison Street to Bishop. Fewer people would notice her there since it's just part of a street—more like an alley.

"Harry Price saw her and thought she was a man. She's pretty tall for a woman, but nobody really knew how tall because she was always sittin'. The wheelchair was the perfect cover. She kept her head down, so nobody saw her face.

"She went to Lucille Harris' back door, knocked and held up the yellow roses. Thinkin' it was a delivery for her, Lucille opened the screen door and invited the delivery 'man' inside. When Lucille took the roses and turned around to set them on the counter, Ruth stabbed her in the back. You know the rest. No need to go through that again.

"She went home the same way she came. She changed back into her bed clothes, hid the bloody clothes and got back on the couch. When Jim woke up about 3:00, she told him she'd slept until 11:30, that the pain pills had knocked her out. He was used to hearin' that, too.

"When he went to work that night at 11:00, she washed the bloody clothes and then hid the bloody knife in Mr. Baxter's chicken house. She wanted him to find it. She wanted Jim to be punished for what he did to her."

"That's a mighty mean woman, if you ask me," said Daddy. "She did a lot of plannin' and figurin' to make all of that happen."

"What if someone had stopped her on the street?" Mama asked.

"She could've said that she was tryin' to deliver some flowers and got turned around. She could've asked for directions."

"Will she be charged in the Texarkana murder, too?" Daddy asked him.

"That's up to the police up there."

"That's all I had to tell you. I just wanted you to know. I'd appreciate it if you'd keep this under your hat for now. It'll all come out soon enough, but it'd be better if you didn't discuss it with anyone until the legal process gets goin'."

"We'll keep quiet," Daddy told him.

"I hate it that we didn't know more before the trial, but Rufus Cornelius figured it out. That turned out good for Jim Tressell," Detective Binotti said.

"I knew Rufus was a smart young man. I'd want him representin' me if I ever need a lawyer," said Daddy.

"Well, let's hope you never do," Mama said and patted him on the arm.

"I best be off now. Are the Mavs gonna be good again this year, Coach?"

"Looks like it. A lot of guys are back from last year."

"We're hopin' to go all the way to state this year," I told him.

"I hope you're right, Bobbi," he said and laughed as he stood up.

Detective Binotti said goodbye to all of us, walked out to his car and drove away.

SEPTEMBER

School started the Tuesday after Labor Day. It was hard to believe that a little over three weeks ago I'd been sitting in a courtroom at Mr. Tressell's trial. Now I was sitting in a hot classroom with a bunch of kids, and my sixth grade teacher was at the black board explaining an arithmetic problem to all of us.

Every day after school Katie, Law and I walked home together, changed into our play clothes and met at the hammock to take turns swinging. Mr. Tressell worked in his garden almost every afternoon. Sometimes he waved to us, and sometimes he even came over to talk to us.

On the Saturday afternoon after Daddy's first football game of the season which the Mavs won by twenty points, Law and I were swinging Katie in the hammock when Mr. Tressell called out to us from his back gate.

"You kids. Come over here," he said.

We stopped swinging the hammock so that Katie could get out, and we ran over to him. He was holding a brown paper sack.

"Hey, Mr. Tressell," I said. He opened the gate that led to his garden.

"Got somethin' for you," he said.

"What is it?" asked Law.

"Presents," he said.

"Presents for us?" asked Katie. "I love presents!"

He opened the sack and handed Law a pocket knife.

"Is this your knife?" Law asked him.

"Had it since I was your age. Want you to have it."

"Thank you. I've never had a knife before."

"Better ask your grandmother how old you have to be before you can carry it."

"I'm old enough now."

"Ask her anyway."

"Yessir," said Law as he put the knife in his pocket.

He handed Katie a silver coin.

"Railroad gave me this. For ten years of hard work."

"It's really shiny," Katie told him. "Thank you a lot."

"It's real silver. Can't spend it. Keep it in a safe place," he told her.

"I will."

He handed me a book. It was about gardens and had a picture of yellow roses on the front.

"About gardens. Grow your own vegetables and flowers one day," he said to me.

"It's a pretty book. Thank you, Mr. Tressell," I said.

"Book I loaned her," he said as he nodded toward Miss Lucille's house.

"This's for you, too. For helpin' me. Want you to have it." He handed me his pocket watch.

"It's a watch," said Law.

"Used it at the railroad. Keeps good time."

"It's so pretty. It's got a really neat chain. Don't you need it anymore?" I asked him, but he was already walking back toward his house. We all watched him go.

"Thank you, Mr. Tressell!" I called out to him.

He didn't turn around.

"I love presents," said Katie. "My coin's really pretty."

"Think your grandmother'll let you carry the knife?" I asked Law.

"If I promise to be careful with it."

"Let's swing some more before it's time to go in," I said. We put our presents on the grass near the hammock.

About an hour later, I heard Mama calling, "Bobbi!"

"See ya at Sunday School tomorrow," I told them as I picked up my book and watch and crossed the street.

Mama was setting the table for supper when I told her about the presents.

She looked surprised. "Mr. Tressell gave you presents? Just now?"

"He called us over to his gate and got 'em out of a paper sack."

"That sure was nice of him. When your daddy and I visited him last week and took him a pie, he didn't have much to say. He's always been so quiet, and he's been through so much these last few months. Poor man."

"What'd he give y'all?" she asked.

"He gave Katie a shiny silver coin that the railroad gave him for workin' hard for ten years. He gave Law his pocket knife. He's had it since he was a boy."

"Show me what he gave you."

"It's a book about gardens. It has yellow roses on the front," I held it up so she could see it. "He said that Miss Lucille used it and that maybe I could grow my own garden one day."

"That's very thoughtful. What a pretty cover!" she said.

"And he gave me a watch, too," I said.

"What?"

"He gave me his pocket watch." I held it up.

She didn't even look at the watch. She dropped the plate she was holding. It broke in half when it hit the floor.

"Watch Betsy!" she yelled as she ran out the back door.

"Where ya goin'?" I called to her, but she was already gone.

I ran to the front window and saw mama running down the street. She stopped at Mr. Tressell's house and ran up to his front door. Then she ran to his backyard and through his garden gate. I waited a while, but I didn't see her anymore.

I picked up the broken plate and swept the floor, but Mama was still gone.

"C'mon, Betsy. Let's play with your blocks. Mama'll be back soon."

⊶+ +⊷

It was starting to get dark, and Mama still wasn't home. I was about to call Mavis to ask her what I should do when Daddy came in the back door.

"Mama's not here. She dropped a plate. It broke, and she ran out the door to Mr. Tressell's house."

"I know," he told me. "Sit down here on the couch so I can tell you about somethin' that happened today."

"Is Mama hurt?"

"Your mama's fine. It's Mr. Tressell. Sometimes people get really down about things and decide they don't want to live anymore. Mr. Tressell's been real sad lately. He took his own life today."

"You mean he died?"

Daddy nodded.

"But he gave us presents just a little while ago."

"That's how your mama knew somethin' was wrong. He gave you kids things that were very special to him. That was his way of sayin' goodbye."

"What'd he do?"

"He went to his garage and stopped up the tail pipe on his truck with some rags. Then he got inside with the motor runnin', and the fumes made him go to sleep. The gas from the fumes is poisonous. You never wanna be in a room or a car with fumes like that. They'll kill you. He didn't wake up."

I started to cry.

Daddy put his arms around me and said, "I'm so sorry, Bobbi girl. You've been through too much for a girl your age. Your mama found him in the garage in his truck when she went over there. She could tell what'd happened, so she called the police. Then she called me at the field house. She'll be home as soon as she can."

"Why'd he do it, Daddy?"

"He's been really sad. It's a terrible thing to be that sad. People that take their life give up and can't bear to keep livin'."

———

Daddy fixed us hot dogs for supper. We were almost finished eating when Mama came in the back door. Her eyes were red, and her face looked tired. We all got up from the table to meet her. While she hugged Daddy, Betsy held onto one of her legs, and I put my arms around her waist.

"You okay, Mama?" I asked.

"I'm all right, honey," she said. "It was so terrible to find him that way."

Daddy rubbed her shoulders. "I'm so sorry you had to be the one. He must've been really down to do somethin' like that."

"I wish we'd known. You know, last week when we were over there, he could've talked to us, but he didn't." She rubbed her eyes. "As soon as Bobbi told me about the watch, I knew somethin' bad was gonna happen. That's why I ran out of here so fast," she said to me. "I was hopin' I could stop him."

"Why'd the watch make you know?" I asked her.

"When you told me about the knife he gave Law and the coin he gave Katie and even the book he gave you, I thought that was his way of sayin' thank you for supportin' him, for bein' in his corner durin' all of this. But when you said he gave you his watch, I knew. A railroad man's pocket watch is his most prized possession. It's always with him. He needs it for his work, so when he gave it to you, that meant he wasn't plannin' on goin' back to work."

"I'm sorry, Mama," I told her.

"Oh, Bobbi, you don't have any reason to be sorry. He wanted you and Katie and Law to have those things that meant somethin' to him. You didn't have anythin' to do with what he did in his garage."

"How'd you know to look there, honey?" Daddy asked her.

"I ran to the front door first and knocked real loud. When he didn't come, I ran around to the backyard and didn't see him. I heard a motor runnin', and I knew. I ran to the garage. I was afraid he might've locked the door, but it opened. I saw him inside slumped over the wheel of his truck. When I opened the door, the fumes almost knocked me down. I pulled him out best I could, but I knew it was too late to save him."

"Oh, honey, I'm so sorry," Daddy said.

"Me, too," I said.

She leaned down and picked up Betsy who had started to cry.

"Let me put Betsy to bed, and I'll tell you the rest."

"I'll fix you a hot dog," said Daddy.

"Maybe later, Jack. Thanks, but I'm not really hungry."

Daddy and I washed the dishes and cleaned up the kitchen. When Mama came back to the den, she told us the rest of what had happened at Mr. Tressell's.

She had called the police. They didn't turn on their sirens because he was already gone. She said they arrived in less than ten minutes. The Justice of the Peace and an ambulance came after that to take him away. Detective Binotti came, too, since he'd been a part of the whole case with Lucille and the trial. He took her statement.

"What's that, Mama?"

"I had to tell them what happened just like I've been tellin' you and Daddy. They wrote it all down. He asked me to come with him while he looked around the house to see if Jim had left any kind of note. A lot of the time when people take their own lives, they leave a note sayin' goodbye or givin' a reason. There was a one page letter—just a couple of sentences—on the kitchen table."

"Did you read it?"

"Detective Binotti read it and told me what it said. We can't tell anybody this, you know."

I nodded.

"He said he was sorry he'd caused two women to be killed. He knew what he'd done with them had been the reason Ruth did what she did. That was all it said. I wish he'd talked to someone—his niece or even Mr. Cornelius."

"It wouldn't have helped, Nita," said Daddy. "The guilt was too much for him. He couldn't live with it."

"I'm so tired," Mama said.

"Let's all get ready for bed. Things'll be better tomorrow."

I hoped Daddy was right.

⚜

The next morning we got dressed for church as we always did on Sunday. Mama was wearing a red dress with a white lace collar. It was Daddy's favorite since red and white were the MHS school colors. I was wearing a pink cotton dress that had my initials embroidered on the collar, and Betsy looked cute in a frilly yellow playsuit.

"I'm a lucky fella. I have the prettiest girls in town goin' to church with me today," Daddy said.

"You're mighty handsome yourself, Jack Rogers," Mama said and kissed him on the cheek.

"I think we'll go in the car today. Would you like that, Bobbi girl?" he asked.

"I sure would. We won't get all sweaty like we do when we walk."

We didn't speak about Mr. Tressell on our way to church, and nobody said anything in my Sunday School class about him either, but when it came time for Brother Rutledge to preach his sermon during the worship service, he talked about Mr. and Mrs. Tressell and Miss Lucille.

"Loved ones, our town has been through a lot these last few months. First we lost one of our newest members, Lucille Harris. You'll remember that Mrs. Harris joined our congregation last December and accepted our invitation to play the piano in our worship services and to lead our children's choir which was without a director. She blessed all of us with her musical abilities, with her kindness to our children and with her pretty smile. Last evening we lost another one of our members. I'm not sure if all of you have heard, but last night Jim Tressell took his own life. These are trying times, for sure, and the best thing we can do is pray for the families and friends of these two members who have departed from our midst.

"Our scripture passage for today's message is found in Romans 12:12-21. Please open your Bibles and stand with me as we read from God's Word:

[12] Rejoicing in hope; patient in tribulation; continuing instant in prayer;
[13] Distributing to the necessity of saints; given to hospitality.
[14] Bless them which persecute you: bless, and curse not.
[15] Rejoice with them that do rejoice, and weep with them that weep.

¹⁶ Be of the same mind one toward another. Mind not high things, but condescend to men of low estate. Be not wise in your own conceits.

¹⁷ Recompense to no man evil for evil. Provide things honest in the sight of all men.

¹⁸ If it be possible, as much as lieth in you, live peaceably with all men.

¹⁹ Dearly beloved, avenge not yourselves, but rather give place unto wrath: for it is written, Vengeance is mine; I will repay, saith the Lord.

²⁰ Therefore if thine enemy hunger, feed him; if he thirst, give him drink: for in so doing thou shalt heap coals of fire on his head.

²¹ Be not overcome of evil, but overcome evil with good."

"You may be seated," he said. "In times of trouble we seek refuge in the words of our Lord. He wants us to rejoice in our hope in Him, to be patient in times of trouble and to pray in all things.

"He reminds us that we need to be ready to help others when they are in need, and as hard as it may be, we need to bless those who persecute us.

"These verses also tell us to be happy with those who are happy and to weep with those who weep, and recent events have certainly provided us opportunities to weep with our friends and neighbors.

"I think that we can look at what's happened over the last several months and see clearly that the Bible tells us we are not to take revenge on another person even when that person has done something to hurt us. You've heard me say many times that you need to read your Bible every day and walk closely with the Lord because the temptations of the world are always trying to pull you away from Him. Even Christian people like Lucille Harris and Jim Tressell can get caught in the web of the world. We never know when a small sin will lead to a big sin.

"Not only should we pray for the families of Lucille and Jim, but we also need to pray for Ruth Tressell who let evil overcome her."

I looked up at Mama. She was dabbing her eyes with a tissue. Daddy was patting her hand. I took her other hand in mine.

Brother Rutledge continued, "How can we overcome the evil that has touched our fair city? The Bible tells us we can overcome evil by doing good—helping our neighbors, sharing in their struggles, reaching out to them in kindness. We cannot allow hate to grow in our hearts for those who wrong us because those feelings of hatred will consume us. Nurturing that hate often leads us to hurt others. The Bible teaches us to forgive others just as Jesus forgives us. I'm not saying this is easy, but forgiving those who have wronged us will take away the bitterness that will build up in us when we don't forgive.

"This world we live in is filled with pitfalls. It's easy for us to judge others when they make mistakes, but it's important to remember that we all have weaknesses. How many times have you said or done something you wish you could take back? All of us have, but as Christians we know God is there for us in the good times and the bad times. He is faithful to forgive us when we fail. He is faithful to encourage us when we're down. He is faithful to comfort us when we weep. We need to pray each day for God's strength to keep us on the right path, to live honorable lives and to treat others as we want to be treated."

After the hymn of invitation and the benediction, everyone stood up to leave. We lined up with the other church members to shake hands with Brother Rutledge.

"Thank you for that sermon today," Mama told him.

He took both of her hands in his and said, "Nita, thank you for being a friend to Lucille and Jim and to Ruth Tressell, too. I appreciate your sweet spirit. You and your family have been through a lot this past year. Thank you for doing good."

Mama smiled and said, "Thank you." Her cheeks were pink.

Daddy shook Brother Rutledge's hand, and the three of us went to the nursery to get Betsy. When we were in the car, Daddy looked at Mama and said, "Brother Rutledge was right, you know. You are a lovin', carin' woman. Both of you girls should be proud to be her daughters."

"You're embarrassin' me, Jack. I was just bein' a friend. Bobbi's the one we should be braggin' on. She never gave up on Jim Tressell when all of us had decided he was guilty."

"That's true enough. I'm proud of you, too, Bobbi," he said, "but there's something else I need to add to all of that."

"What's that, Daddy?"

He looked at Mama, then at me and then at Betsy and asked, "Don't you girls think I'm the best husband and daddy in the whole world?"

He started laughing, and we all laughed with him as he drove us home from church.

⊷≺┼ ┼≻⊶

Mr. Tressell's graveside service was on Wednesday at 4:00. Daddy, Mr. Cornelius and Mr. Tressell's T & P Railroad crew who testified at his trial were the pallbearers.

As we were walking over to the white tent that was set up at Colonial Cemetery, Mr. Tressell's niece, Susan, motioned to us and asked Mama, Betsy and me to sit with her on the front row in front of the casket. Katie and Mavis joined us there.

There wasn't a large crowd at the service. Some other men from T & P Railroad came over to speak to Susan Tressell. All of our neighbors were there—Mr. and Mrs. Van Worth and Lottie, Mrs. Lawrence and Law, Charla and Roy Ed Peteet, Mr. and Mrs. Sewell, Tada and Nona Baxter and Colonel and Mrs. Alton. Katie's dad was at the back of the tent holding Annie. I saw Harry Price standing next to him. He was talking as usual. When Harry saw me, he waved. I waved back.

As Brother Rutledge took his place in front of the casket to start the graveside service, I saw a police car pull up and park. Detective Binotti got out and started walking toward the tent. He was carrying a vase of yellow roses.

EPILOGUE
AUGUST 2009

I hadn't been back to Rusk Street in over forty years. In 1962, Daddy was offered a coaching job at a bigger school in Waco, so we left Marshall. I graduated from Waco High School and attended Baylor University. Since I had never lived anywhere but Texas, I applied to law school at the University of Southern California, was accepted and met my husband in our Constitutional Law class. After we graduated, we married and moved to San Jose where he had grown up. We've been there ever since. Our daughter and four grandchildren live close by. My sister Betsy and her family live in Houston. We lost Daddy in 2003 and Mama two years later in 2005. They were in assisted living near Betsy and were big football fans until the end.

Katie went to the University of Texas and then moved to Santa Fe. She's an artist and teaches in a private school. Even as a child she loved to paint. Law graduated from Sam Houston State and majored in criminal justice. He was in the Secret Service and then the FBI. He retired last year. I keep in touch with both of them through our annual Christmas cards.

On this hot August day, I was back in Marshall to litigate a patent trial in this plaintiff friendly town where 78% of the cases that reach trial result in plaintiff wins. It wasn't unusual for two California companies whose offices were only blocks from one another in San Jose to end up fighting a patent battle in Marshall's federal courthouse.

My team hadn't arrived yet, so I decided to drive through my old neighborhood on Rusk Street. Forty plus years had not been kind to this part of town. A condemned notice was taped the Baxters' house, and their large wrap-around porch had collapsed. Tall weeds grew in the yard where the Lawrences once lived, and my childhood home was badly in need of a complete remodeling job. The pretty pink shutters and matching shingles were long gone, and the front yard was now a dirt parking lot for two pickup trucks.

Most of the houses on Rusk Street looked sad, but the house on the corner where Miss Lucille had lived looked clean and neat and had beautiful yellow roses growing in front of the porch. I felt drawn to them. I parked my car next to the curb. As I crossed the street, a tall woman with gray hair and blue eyes opened the door and stepped out onto her porch to check her mailbox.

She saw me walking toward her and waved. She had a friendly smile.

"Looking for someone?" she asked.

"I don't mean to bother you, but I grew up on Rusk Street. I saw your yellow roses. They're beautiful," I said.

"I get lots of compliments on them."

"I'm sure you do. I used to live in the house next door—just across the vacant lot there. It was much prettier then."

"With pink shutters and pink shingles," she said.

"That's right."

"You must be one of Nita Rogers' daughters?"

"I'm Bobbi, the older one."

"You may not remember me, but I remember you. I'm Susan Kendall. Jim Tressell was my uncle. "

"My goodness. It's been such a long time."

"Won't you come in?"

"Are you sure I'm not intruding?" I asked.

"Not at all. I was about to have a Coke. Can I get you one?"

"I would love one."

"Have a seat on the couch. I'll be right back."

I sat down on her brown leather sofa and looked around the room. The walls were cream, and her drapes were a pretty floral pattern in red, green, tan and yellow. The room seemed very comfortable, but it also seemed so much smaller than I remembered. There was an upright piano against one wall, and on the pretty oak coffee table were three books about gardening and flowers. On the end table next to the sofa were several family photos. I recognized one I had seen many years ago on a shelf at the Tressells' house. I picked it up as she returned with the Cokes.

"That's Uncle Jim and me. I was always crazy about him. He taught me how to garden."

"His garden seemed so big to me back then."

"It was a big garden, and he was so proud of it. He loved to share his tomatoes."

"He used to bring them to our July the 4th picnics. Such good memories of simpler times."

"And some not so good ones, too," she said. "With this house's history, you're probably wondering why I'm living here."

I nodded.

"When Uncle Jim died, he left instructions in his will that I should sell his house and his truck—I wouldn't have kept that truck for any reason after what happened—and take the money and buy this house on the corner. The will said that I didn't have to live in the house. I could lease it out, but he wanted me to plant yellow roses in the front yard. He asked me to make sure that someone looked after the yard and the roses. I moved in all those years ago and took it upon myself to make sure the roses looked pretty— as a tribute to him, and to her, Lucille—for him. He must've really loved her."

She paused remembering.

"You know, your mother was one of the sweetest people I ever met. She was so kind to me after Uncle Jim died. Helped me pack up all of their things, and we had some good, long talks. I always hated that she was the one who found him. She helped Aunt Ruth, too, before everything came out about her killing Lucille and Linda Lou."

"We were still living here when she entered a guilty plea to avoid a trial. Where's Ruth now?"

"She died in 1986 from heart problems. I wasn't sure Aunt Ruth even had a heart to tell you the truth—so much hate in her. I tried to visit her a few times after she was arrested and after Uncle Jim killed himself, but she wouldn't have anything to do with me. She served twenty-five years of her life sentence before she died. She's buried next to Uncle Jim. He owned two plots at Colonial Cemetery. That didn't seem right to me, but she didn't have any other family."

It was time for me to head to the hotel to meet my team, so I thanked Susan for the Coke and told her how much I enjoyed the visit. As she walked me to the front door, she said, "If you're ever back in Marshall, please stop by again. Just look for the yellow roses."

My cell phone rang as I was walking to my car. I recognized my daughter's ring tone and stopped to get the phone out of my shoulder bag.

"Hey, honey...yes, the flight was smooth. It's really hot here, hotter than I remembered...I've been by to see my old neighborhood...sad really...I'll tell you more when I get back...will do...hug the kids for me...I love you, too, Lucille."

I put my phone away, turned the car around and drove down Rusk Street toward town.

AUTHOR BIOGRAPHY

Penny Carlile was born in Marshall, Texas, and grew up, not co-incidentally, on Rusk Street. She and her husband now split their time between Marshall and Naples, Florida.

Carlile earned her bachelor of arts in English and speech from Baylor University in 1973. She taught junior high school before she cofounded a direct sales company with her husband. It was during her time as president of the company that she wrote her first book, *Points from Penny*.

The Girl on Rusk Street is fiction, but many of the events in the book are straight out of Carlile's own childhood.

CPSIA information can be obtained
at www.ICGtesting.com
Printed in the USA
LVOW03s2134260418
574991LV00012B/877/P